TURNING BACK TO THE BOX, I began prying the lid off. Kristi crept closer, and when I finally got it open, she screamed at the sight of its contents.

"It's a dead girl!" she cried.

She startled me so much that I hurled the box into the weeds and backed away from it, terrified.

"I saw it, I saw its face!" Kristi was kneeling in the weeds, her hands over her eyes. "Oh, Ashley, what should we do?"

My heart was thumping and I could hardly breathe, but I forced myself to look at what had fallen from the box. Too small to be a person, it lay in the weeds, face down, its clothing in rags, its hair tangled.

Cautiously I reached out and turned it over. Its china face was pale and smudged with dirt. One eye was half-open and the other was closed, its nose was chipped, but it was still beautiful.

I held it toward Kristi. "It's an old doll," I whispered.

Other novels by
Mary Downing Hahn

MARY DOWNING HAHN

THE DOLL IN THE GARDEN

a ghost story

CLARION BOOKS
HOUGHTON MIFFLIN HARCOURT
Boston   New York

Clarion Books
3 Park Avenue
New York, New York 10016

Copyright © 1989 by Mary Downing Hahn

Clarion Books is an imprint of
Houghton Mifflin Harcourt Publishing Company.

hmhbooks.com

The text was set in Galliard.
Cover design by Kaitlin Yang

Library of Congress cataloging-in-publication data is available.

ISBN: 978-0-89919-848-4 hardcover
ISBN: 978-0-618-87315-9 paperback

Manufactured in the United States of America
DOC 10 9 8 7 6 5 4 3 2 1
4500800854

For my nieces, Sarah and Lisa Collins,
and
my cousin Colleen Nugent

Contents

Chapter 1

The Cat Hater

THE DAY WE MOVED into Monkton Mills, I made an enemy of our new landlady. My mother and I were renting the top floor of what had once been a big single-family house, and the owner, Miss Cooper, was sitting on the front porch when we arrived in our rented truck. She watched us walk up the sidewalk toward the house, and the first thing she said was, "What's in there?"

She was speaking to me, but she was looking at the plastic cat carrier I was toting.

"It's my cat Oscar," I said, trying hard not to stare at her. Miss Cooper was the oldest human being I'd ever seen. Her face was furrowed with wrinkles, and her nose jutted out like a hawk's beak, sharp and cruel. The hand grasping her cane was knotted with veins, and her collarbones stuck out above the loose neckline of her flowered dress.

The real estate agent who'd helped us find a place we could afford had warned Mom and me that Miss Cooper wasn't very friendly and didn't particularly like children. So, hoping to soften the old woman's heart, I smiled politely at her. "Would you like to see him?"

"Certainly not!" Miss Cooper levered herself up from her rocking chair, and the old dog sleeping beside her got up too and growled. He was black and not very big, but he had a sharp, pointed nose and a mean look around the eyes.

"I detest cats," Miss Cooper went on. "You take that creature upstairs right now and don't ever let me see it in the yard. If it kills one bird, I'll send it straight to the pound!"

"Grrrr," said the dog who obviously hated cats as much as his mistress did.

I looked at Mom. She was shifting her heavy typewriter case from one hand to the other, her face worried. "I'm Jan Cummings." She stuck out her free hand and smiled, but Miss Cooper merely stared at her.

"And this is Ashley," Mom continued, her smile fading. "I'm sorry you weren't here the day Mrs. Walker showed me the apartment."

"Ashley." Miss Cooper turned back to me and sniffed. "What kind of name is that? It doesn't sound proper for a girl." She poked her face closer to mine. "How old are you?"

"Almost eleven," I said, backing off a little. Up close, she was kind of scary.

"Almost? That means ten, if you ask me." Miss Cooper frowned, adding even more creases to her forehead, and the dog moved a little closer, sniffing at Oscar's carrier. "Well, I'm eighty-eight, and I know what girls your age are like," she went on. "Don't think you can get away with anything just because I'm old. There's nothing wrong with my eyes or my ears, missy."

"Don't worry about Ashley," Mom said. Putting her arm around my shoulders, she drew me close. "She won't give you any trouble."

Miss Cooper turned her attention to Mom. "Where's Mr. Cummings?" she asked.

Mom's face reddened. "It's just Ashley and me," she said calmly.

"Divorced?" Miss Cooper leaned toward us, taking in every detail: Mom's tall, thin figure, her long brown hair, her faded jeans, her old tee shirt, and me, a smaller version of Mom right down to my freckles and worn-out running shoes. Then she sniffed and turned away. "Come on, Max," she snapped at the dog who was growling at the pet carrier.

Two steps later, she looked back. "I don't want a lot of noise up there," she said. "I'll complain to the real estate company if my sleep is disturbed."

We stood where we were and watched the old woman shuffle inside and slam the door behind her. In the sudden silence, Mom and I looked at each other.

"Well," Mom said, "so much for a friendly welcome." With a sigh, she followed the sidewalk around the corner to a steep flight of stairs at the back of the house. They were more like a fire escape than anything else, and I was glad we didn't have much more furniture; the movers had brought the heavy things earlier. But getting the little that was left up to our apartment wasn't going to be easy.

Mom paused on the porch at the top of the steps. "Isn't the lawn lovely?" she asked.

I stared down at the neatly mown expanse of grass that swept away from the house. In its center was a circular bed of bright flowers. Bird feeders hung from several trees, and a pair of catbirds splashed in a stone bath.

In sharp contrast, an overgrown mass of shrubbery and towering weeds cast a shadow across the end of the yard. It must have been a rose garden once, but, from the look of it, the bushes had grown wild for years. Honeysuckle, wild flowers, and weeds struggled together to reach the sun.

Tall hedges bordered both sides of the lawn, but from the porch I could see across them. Next door was a big white house similar to Miss Cooper's, trimmed with fancy woodwork and graced with porches front and back, well-tended despite the bicycles in the driveway. On the other side was an empty lot, grown high with Queen Anne's lace and black-eyed Susans.

"Can I let Oscar out of his carrier now?" I asked Mom. He was meowing and sticking his paw through the bars like a prisoner in a jail movie.

"Put him in your room and close the door, Ash," Mom said. "We don't want him to run outside while we're carrying things in."

My room was at the back of the house, and from my windows I could see the yard, the garden, and the empty field next door. Way beyond were the mountains, hazy blue against the sky. It all seemed very peaceful, and I was glad we'd come to Monkton Mills. Mom and I needed a place like this, I thought. In a new town, far away from everything that reminded us of Daddy, maybe we could stop feeling sad.

To keep myself from thinking about my father, I turned away from the window and opened the door of the pet carrier. "Come on out," I told Oscar.

For a minute Oscar looked at me as if he thought I was playing a trick on him. Then he crept forward and stared at his new surroundings. Ignoring my caress, he slid out from under my hand and ran around the empty room, meowing continuously and staying close to the walls, his belly almost dragging along the floor. Finding nothing to hide under, he darted back into his carrier and crouched at the back.

Mom opened my door a crack and looked at the cat. "Poor old Oscar," she said. "Just leave him in there and come help, Ash. He needs time to get used to moving."

*

Mom and I made at least six trips up the steps to get our things into the apartment. To make it worse, Max barked every time we went up and down the stairs. When we were finally finished, it was late in the afternoon and we were hot and tired and Mom still had to take the rental truck back to Baltimore.

"Why don't you just stay here and rest, Ash?" Mom suggested. "I'll pick up a pizza on the way home, and we can eat it on the porch."

After Mom left, I sat down on the top step. A gentle breeze stirred the bushes in the garden, and I breathed in the sweet fragrance of honeysuckle and roses.

Sitting there, staring at the jungle at the end of the lawn, I wondered why Miss Cooper had let her garden grow wild. The rest of her yard was so neat and tidy. Every bush had been trimmed into a cone or a ball and surrounded by a circle of pine mulch. The flower bed was edged with white stones, and the flowers themselves were laid out in patterns according to size and color.

But the garden was a wilderness, and the more I looked at it, the more inviting it seemed. Lush and green, the bushes swayed in the breeze, promising cool shade and privacy. It was a place to be alone, a place of secrets, a forest for me to explore and make my own.

But not now. I was too hot and tired to move. Lazily I told myself I'd save the garden for tomorrow when I felt more energetic. Yawning, I closed my eyes and stretched. But when I looked at the garden again, I saw a flash of white in the weeds. Was it a cat?

Remembering Miss Cooper's attitude toward Oscar, I forgot my fatigue and ran down the steps. If a cat had ventured into the yard, I'd rescue it before the old woman saw it and called the pound.

As I dashed across the grass, I had the strongest feeling that someone was watching me; I could almost feel eyes boring into the back of my neck. Afraid Miss Cooper had spotted the cat, I glanced over my shoulder. The shades at her windows were drawn and there was no sign of her or Max, but next door I glimpsed a flash of red in the leaves of a tall tree.

Stopping for a moment, I stared hard, sure it wasn't a bird, but I couldn't see a face or even a leg or an arm, just a bit of red that didn't belong there.

"Nosy, aren't you?" I muttered.

A mockingbird answered, and a cat meowed from somewhere in the garden. Reminded of my purpose, I turned my back on the spy, ducked my head to avoid the thorny arm of a rosebush, and pushed my way through the weeds into the cool, green shade of the garden.

Chapter 2

Kristi

ALL AROUND ME roses ran riot, sending long prickly shoots in every direction, fighting with honeysuckle for growing space. Waist-high thistles and Queen Anne's lace almost choked out the daisies and black-eyed Susans.

Hoping I wasn't stepping in poison ivy, I made my way down a narrow path to the dried-up goldfish pond at the center of the garden. In its middle was a statue of a cherub. His arms were draped with ivy and a wreath of honeysuckle circled his head. At his feet were foot-high weeds. His worn features and weather-streaked face reminded me of statues in pictures of Pompeii that I'd seen in a book.

As the stillness of the garden settled around me, I looked for the cat. Calling softly, I thought I heard something rustling in the weeds.

"Kitty, kitty," I whispered, almost sure I saw a pair of green eyes peering out at me. "Kitty, kitty, kitty," I called again. Dropping to my knees, I peered under a rosebush and stretched out my hand.

For a moment, a cool, pink nose brushed against my finger tips. Then it was gone and the garden was empty, silent except for a cloud of gnats circling my head.

"Where did you go?" I tried to crawl into the bushes after the cat, but thorns caught in my hair and thistles pricked my bare arms. Backing out, I sat on the edge of the empty pond. The cherub looked sadly down at me, and a mockingbird hopped from one branch of a dogwood tree to another just over my head.

Where I sat, I was completely surrounded by a dense wall of bushes, trees, and weeds bound together with honeysuckle. Just as I'd thought, the garden was a secret place, somewhere to go when I needed to be alone. No one could see me here – not the spy in the red shirt, not Miss Cooper, not her dog. Not even Mom.

As still as the cherub behind me, I watched the leaves sway in the breeze. Sunlight and shadow mottled the ground, and the weeds whispered to themselves, lulling me like distant voices of children at play. Closing my eyes, I pretended I was in a magical place, safe from pain and sadness and death. In this garden, Daddy was alive again. I could almost hear his voice, smell his pipe and the after-shave lotion he used, feel his hand on my shoulder.

Slowly I opened my eyes like Sleeping Beauty in an enchanted bower, but all I saw were weeds and bushes. Daddy wasn't there. Except for the mockingbird, I was alone. Blinking hard to keep from crying, I got to my feet and tried calling the cat once more.

I thought I heard a faint meow from somewhere deep in the bushes, but the cat wouldn't come to me.

I waited for a few minutes, hoping the cat would change his mind, but when I saw no sign of him, I made my way through the weeds and bushes to the lawn. Mom would be back soon, I thought, and I didn't want to worry her by not being where she'd left me.

As I passed the tree between Miss Cooper's house and the house next door, I saw a girl in a red polo shirt standing in a gap in the hedge. She was younger than I was – seven or eight, I guessed. Her hair was short and shaggy and streaked with yellow from the summer sun, and her skin was golden tan. Her bare feet and legs were dirty and scratched, and she was covered with mosquito bites.

"Are you going to live in Miss Cooper's house?" the girl wanted to know. When I nodded, she said, "My name's Kristi Smith. What's yours?"

"Ashley Cummings," I told her.

She smiled then, a grin that showed the gap between her two front teeth, and started firing questions at me. In a few seconds, she'd learned I was almost eleven; I used to live near Baltimore; I liked reading, drawing, and bike riding; I didn't have a dog but I did have a cat. Finally she got to the question I'd been dreading.

"Where's your dad?" she wanted to know.

"He died last November," I said. "He had cancer." I turned away then, hoping she wouldn't ask me anything else. It was still hard to talk about my father.

Kristi was silent for a while. The only sound was a bird singing in the garden. Finally she cleared her throat and said, "My grandfather died a couple of weeks ago."

I looked at her and she looked at me. It was a long look and it said we understood something about each other. Then Kristi leaned toward me. "How do you like Miss Cooper?"

"Not much," I said. "She hates me already. And my cat too."

"Miss Cooper hates *everybody*," Kristi said. "She calls the police if my brother turns his stereo on after ten. She thinks I'm a nosy brat, and she's always complaining to my mother about me. She says I spy on her."

"Do you?"

"Sometimes." Kristi grinned again. "When I was little I thought she was a witch."

"She looks like one." I thought of Miss Cooper's wild white hair floating around her face, her sharp nose and little chin, her red-rimmed eyes netted with wrinkles.

"I feel sorry for you, living upstairs from her," Kristi went on. "It used to be her house, all of it. She was born there, my mom says, but when she got older she was so poor she had to make the upstairs into an apartment. Nobody lives in it for long, though."

"Why? Because Miss Cooper's so grouchy?"

Kristi put a piece of grass in her mouth and chewed on it. "That's part of the reason," she said after a while.

I watched her for a few seconds, waiting for her to go on. "What's the other reason?" I asked.

"I don't know if I should tell you." As Kristi spoke, she glanced at the garden, then looked away. The shadows were getting longer now, and the tangled underbrush looked dark and mysterious. "You might get scared and want to move away."

I leaned toward Kristi, my face inches from hers. "I won't be scared."

"Well, it's the garden," she said slowly. "Some people think it's haunted."

"A *haunted* garden?" I sat back on my heels and tossed my hair. "How can a garden be haunted?"

Kristi frowned and her lower lip crept out. I could tell she was annoyed at not being taken seriously. "You wait," she muttered. "When you see the cat and hear the crying, you won't laugh."

I stared at her. "What cat?"

"A white one. He meows and meows and then he disappears into the garden. You hear him mostly at night. And only in the summer."

Before I could tell Kristi I'd just seen a white cat, a teenaged boy stepped out on the porch next door. "Hey, Kristi," he called. "Get over here. It's dinnertime."

"That's my brother Brian, the creep," Kristi said. "I have to go. I'll see you tomorrow. Okay?"

She ran through the gap in the hedge, but paused once to call back, "If you hear anybody crying tonight, just remember I told you so." Then she was up her steps and gone, letting the screen door bang shut behind her.

Chapter 3

The White Cat

LEFT ALONE, I ran up the steps and into the empty apartment. Coaxing Oscar into my lap, I stared out the window at the garden. I had seen a white cat, I was sure I had, but he was every bit as real as Oscar. I'd felt his nose, my fingertips had brushed his fur, I'd heard him meow. He couldn't have been a ghost.

But where had he gone? How had he just disappeared? Little goose bumps chased themselves up and down my neck as I tried to convince myself that Kristi was teasing me. She'd watched me go into the garden, she'd probably seen the white cat, and she'd wanted to scare me with ghost stories. That's all there was to it.

*

By the time Mom came home, I was thinking more about pizza than the garden or the white cat. When I heard her car in the driveway, I leaned over the porch railing to watch her balancing the pizza box and a couple of cans of soda.

"Do you need any help?" I called.

Mom shook her head, but I ran down to meet her anyway and took the sodas. The pizza smelled so wonderful I could almost taste the gooey, melted cheese and the hot tomato sauce.

Making ourselves comfortable on the steps, we divided the pizza. The sun had sunk behind the mountains, but the sky was still pink and the shadow of the garden stretched halfway across the lawn. The first star hung just below the moon. Crickets chirped from their hiding places, and a mockingbird sang a long, lovely serenade from the tree in Kristi's yard.

"Baltimore was like an oven," Mom said after we'd eaten enough pizza to take the edge off our appetites. "I was caught right in the middle of rush hour, and the traffic was awful."

"They don't have rush hour here," I told her. "Not enough people."

"Not enough rush either," Mom said. "Just peace and quiet."

I chewed my last piece of pizza and wondered if I should tell Mom what I'd learned from Kristi. I opened my mouth, but when I started talking I told her about meeting Kristi instead. Why ruin a beautiful evening talking about ghosts?

"Maybe you'll make friends with Kristi's mother," I said.

"I didn't come here to make friends, sweetie," Mom said. "I have to finish my dissertation so I can get a job teaching. The money Daddy left won't last forever."

I nodded, but I didn't agree with her. Like me, Mom had been sad for too long. She needed somebody to cheer her up, to make her happy again. I wanted her to smile and laugh and joke the way she used to before Daddy got sick.

I didn't say anything, though; I just leaned against her and felt the comfort of her arm circling me and drawing me close.

*

It wasn't till I'd gotten into bed and turned out the light that I thought about the garden and Kristi's ghost story. The moon shone in my window and slanted across my bed, and a night breeze brought the smell of roses and honeysuckle into the room. Outside, leaves rustled, but I didn't hear anything else. No sobbing, no strange cat meowing – just the sound of Mom's fingers hitting the keys of her typewriter. Feeling sure Kristi had been teasing me, I drifted off to sleep.

Much later I woke up. The house was silent, and Oscar was crouched on the windowsill at the foot of my bed. His body was tense, his ears cocked forward, and his tail lashed back and forth furiously. As I sat up, I heard him growl softly, not at me but at something outside.

Cautiously, I peeked out the window. At first I saw nothing but the moonlight whitening the grass and blackening the shadows. Then something moved near the garden, and Oscar growled again.

It was the white cat. He was creeping along the edge of a shadow, but while I watched, he paused and looked up at my window. The moonlight reflected in his eyes, making them two silver disks. When he meowed softly, Oscar lunged against the screen, tearing at the wire with his claws and growling.

Grabbing my cat, I pulled him away from the window, but he writhed free and disappeared under the bed, still growling. As Oscar vanished, I looked fearfully outside. The white cat was gone, but the scraggly bushes moved with the breeze and the shadows they cast swayed on the grass. The sweet smell of roses filled my room, and I shivered as a gust of wind blew over me.

Before I could crawl under the covers, I heard something in the darkness. It wasn't the breeze in the leaves or a cat meowing or a night bird calling; it was unmistakably the sound of a child crying.

Truly afraid, I pulled the blanket over my head and fought against a strong urge to run to my mother's room and the safety of her bed. As if he sensed my feelings, Oscar came out from his hiding place. Purring in my ear, he curled up on my pillow, and the two of us finally fell asleep together.

Chapter 4

In Trouble

IN THE MORNING, I asked Mom if she'd heard any strange noises during the night.

She smiled and shook her head. "I was up till two typing," she said, "and when I hit the bed, I slept like the proverbial log, Ash."

As Mom paused to sip her coffee, her eyes scanned my face. "People often hear strange noises when they sleep in a new place," she said. "It's perfectly natural."

"But it sounded like a child crying," I told her, "all by itself somewhere outside."

Mom put down her empty cup. "Maybe one of our neighbors has a baby, Ash."

"I saw a cat, too, staring at the house. Oscar was scared of him. He growled and hid under the bed."

Mom looked puzzled. "There's nothing unusual about seeing a cat in the yard. Or in Oscar being scared of him. Oscar's afraid of his own shadow."

Then she reached out and closed her hand over mine. Giving me a squeeze, she said, "How about helping me put up the curtains and pictures?"

Instead of telling Mom what Kristi had told me, I silently finished my cereal. In the morning sunlight, the garden had lost its sinister quality, and I found myself thinking again of building my own little hideout in its shady center. Unlike Kristi, I wouldn't be scared away by a white cat, especially not in the daytime.

*

When we'd finished hanging the curtains and pictures in their new places, I told Mom I was going to visit Kristi. But, as I ran across the grass, Miss Cooper stopped me.

Without giving me a chance to say hello, she said, "Did I see you in my garden yesterday?"

I nodded, surprised by her tone of voice. It hadn't occurred to me she wouldn't want me in the garden. "The real estate agent said I could play in the backyard," I told her.

"Not in the garden, though. Not there! You stay away from my roses!"

"It's all weeds," I began, but Miss Cooper interrupted me.

"Don't you sass me! This is my house and if I

don't want you and your mother here, I can kick you out – just like that!" Miss Cooper snapped her fingers with a dry sound like sandpaper being rubbed together.

As if to emphasize what Miss Cooper said, Max bared his teeth and growled at me.

"And I don't want that Smith girl in my yard. Or her brother – do you hear me?" Miss Cooper added shrilly.

"Kristi's my friend," I said, edging away from her. By now I could feel the hedge at my back. A few more steps and I'd be safe from Miss Cooper and her dog.

"We'll see about that!" She brandished her walking stick and turned away from me. I watched her pause at the bottom of our steps. "Is your mother home?" she called.

Before I could answer, Mom came outside and leaned over the railing. "Is something wrong, Miss Cooper?"

Without waiting to hear what the old woman would tell Mom, I ran through the gap in the hedge to Kristi's house.

When I knocked at the door, Kristi's mother invited me in. Her brother was sitting at the kitchen table reading the comics, but he barely looked up at me.

"So you're Ashley," Mrs. Smith said, smiling pleasantly. "Kristi's upstairs doing some chores, but she'll be down soon."

Mrs. Smith offered me a seat and a glass of Hi-C. While I sipped it, she told me she had a pie in the oven. "I was planning to send Kristi over with it, but maybe you can take it to your mother yourself."

Brian groaned. "I thought you were making that for us," he said. Close up, he was a taller version of Kristi – same tawny hair, same tan skin, same gap between his front teeth.

"I made two," Mrs. Smith said. "One for Ashley and her mother and one for us."

Brian wrinkled his nose as if he were thinking half a pie was more than enough for Mom and me. Then he pushed his chair away from the table and left the room. I could hear him whistling as he thumped upstairs.

"Teenagers," Mrs. Smith sighed as she gathered up Brian's breakfast dishes and dumped them in the sink.

Glancing out the kitchen window, she watched Miss Cooper and my mother for a few seconds. "Don't let that old grouch worry you," Mrs. Smith said to me. "She doesn't have much use for children, so I always tell Kristi and Brian to stay out of her way as much as possible. Of course, that only makes them devil her all the more."

Just then Kristi came downstairs, and I followed

her outside. She led me up a ladder into her tree house, and I realized that's where she'd been sitting when I saw her red shirt the day before. The tree house had been hammered together from all kinds and sizes of wood and it tilted to one side. But it had a roof and two crooked windows, and it was big enough for us to stand up in.

"Brian built this when he was ten, but he gave it to me a couple of years ago," Kristi said. "One of these days, if my dad ever buys me the paint, I'm going to fix it up. Mom might even make some curtains for the windows."

As Kristi droned on about her plans for the tree house, I interrupted her. After all, I'd come over here to talk about something much more important than paint and curtains and rugs. "Were you trying to scare me last night?" I asked her.

Kristi sucked in her breath and her eyes widened. "You heard the ghost, too, didn't you?" she whispered.

"It was you," I said. "Playing a trick on me."

Kristi shook her head. "It was not! Whenever I hear that sound, it scares me to death. I hide under the covers and put my fingers in my ears."

"I don't believe you." I glared at Kristi. No seven-year-old kid was going to scare me.

For a couple of minutes, Kristi didn't say anything. She just sat there on the platform and scratched the mosquito bites on her legs. Then she looked past me at the garden. "I don't care what you think, Ashley," she said. "Every summer the cat comes and I hear the crying – why would I make up something like that?"

"For a joke, to tease me or scare me."

Kristi shook her head. "I don't want to scare you," she said and her face got red. "I want you to be my friend. Honest."

I looked her in the eye for as long as I could without blinking, but she kept her eyes on mine, and she didn't blink either. Little goose bumps ran up and down my spine and made me shiver.

"So what do you think is going on?" I asked her. "Why would a garden be haunted?"

Kristi shook her head and together we stared down at the tangled bushes and weeds. From here, I couldn't see the little cherub or the dried-up goldfish pond, but I noticed a movement in the shrubbery near the garden's center, and I wondered if the white cat was back. I wanted to see him again in the daylight. He had to be real, I thought, a stray cat who'd made a home for himself in the underbrush.

"Will you go in the garden with me?" I asked Kristi. "I want to find the white cat and prove he's real."

She chewed on her lip and stared at me for a second before busying herself by scratching another mosquito bite. "I'm not going in there," she said in a low voice.

"Are you scared?"

"No!" Kristi scowled at me, the mosquito bite forgotten. "I just don't want to."

I leaned toward her. "Come with me and prove you're not scared."

"Miss Cooper will see us," Kristi muttered.

"Not if we're careful. I bet we can sneak into the garden from your yard."

When Kristi once more returned her attention to her mosquito bites, I added, "It's not scary in the daytime. It's nice and cool. There's a goldfish pool in the middle, and I was thinking we could fix it up and make it our secret hideout. Wouldn't that be neat?"

"We already have my tree house," Kristi said. "Can't it be our special place?"

I sprang to my feet, exasperated. "All right," I said. "If you won't help me, I'll do it by myself."

Without looking at Kristi, I started backing down the rope ladder. But, before I reached the ground, I heard her behind me, begging me to wait.

Chapter 5

The Garden's Secret

JUST AS KRISTI and I hit the ground under the tree house, Mrs. Smith stepped out on her back porch, holding a cherry pie.

"I'd deliver it myself," Mrs. Smith told me, "but I'm right in the middle of doing the wash. You tell your mother to come over, though, as soon as she gets a chance. I'd love to meet her."

"Are you sure it's okay if I come with you?" Kristi said as she followed me through the gap in the hedge. "I heard what Miss Cooper said about me being in the yard."

I looked at Miss Cooper's windows, but as usual all the shades were pulled down. "You can visit me," I said. "It's our apartment, and we can invite anybody we want."

As we started up the steps, I heard Max barking from somewhere inside the house. "Does he bite?" I asked Kristi.

"Mad Max? He's getting kind of old now, and Mom says his bark is worse than his bite." She glanced down as if she expected to see Max coming up the stairs after us. "I don't think I'd take any chances with him, though."

Mom was delighted with the pie and happy to meet Kristi. She told her she'd come over soon. But the minute she'd eaten her piece of pie, she excused herself and went back to her typewriter.

"Come on," I said to Kristi. "Let's explore the garden now."

Without giving her a chance to argue, I ran down the steps. Glancing at Miss Cooper's windows, I saw the blinds were still drawn. Recklessly I sprinted across the grass and plunged into the garden's cool, green shade.

In a few seconds I heard Kristi pushing her way cautiously through the undergrowth. When she emerged, her face was red and shiny from the heat, and she was breathing hard as she sank down on the pond's edge beside me.

"It's spooky in here," Kristi whispered. Peering into the shadowy spaces under the bushes, she added, "I know that white cat's hiding somewhere, just waiting to get me."

For some reason, probably because of Kristi's talk of ghosts, the garden seemed a little scary to me, too, but I wasn't going to admit it. Brushing a cobweb away from my face, I said, "Just think, nobody can see us in here. Not even Miss Cooper. It's our private kingdom, Kristi. We can be princesses here."

Kristi sighed and looked at the cherub's worn face. "He looks sad," she said, "like he's been crying."

She was right. Years of rain had made streaks on the cherub's face like the tracks of tears. To add to the melancholy, a mourning dove began to coo, and a cloud drifted in front of the sun, casting everything into deep gray shade.

"Let's go to my house," Kristi said. "We can play with my Barbie dolls."

I shook my head. "Go home if you want to, but I'm staying here."

Without looking at her, I stepped into the pond and started tugging at the ivy and honeysuckle draping the cherub.

For a few minutes Kristi watched me silently. Then, without saying a word, she sighed loudly and yanked a handful of weeds out of the pond.

Even with Kristi's help, it was hot, dirty work. The sun popped out from behind the clouds again, and in no time we were both sweating. Mosquitoes whined around our heads and gnats tried to get in our eyes, but we kept on working till the cherub was free of ivy and honeysuckle and the pond was weed-free.

"Maybe we could run a hose out here from your yard and fill up the pond," I said.

"And buy some fishes for it," Kristi said.

I nodded, glad to hear a little enthusiasm in her voice.

Even though Kristi wanted to stop and rest, I talked her into clearing a circle around the pond. While I was dumping an armload of weeds by the fence, I suddenly heard her scream. Startled, I ran to her side and stared into a hole she'd made pulling out a gigantic thistle.

"There's something buried here." Kristi pointed a wobbly finger at the corner of a wooden box sticking out of the dirt. Her face had turned white under her tan, giving her skin a grayish look, and she was shaking.

Except for the persistent cooing of the mourning dove, it was so quiet I could almost hear my own heart beating. "It's not deep enough to be a grave," I whispered.

As a worm coiled itself out of the dirt and wriggled away, I said, "Maybe it's a treasure chest." My voice was so loud it made Kristi jump.

Cautiously, I knelt down and gently brushed the dirt away from the plain wood box. It wasn't very big. Maybe sixteen to twenty inches long, no more than three or four inches deep, and six inches wide.

"Look, there's something carved on the top." Spitting on my finger, I cleaned the dirt from the letters crudely scratched into the lid. "I think it says *Anna Maria,*" I said, but Kristi was standing too far away to see.

"Bury it again, Ashley, just the way it was," she begged. "It's the white cat's coffin, I know it is!"

But something in me wanted to see what was in the box. Telling myself I was going to find gold or silver, enough to make Mom and me rich for life, I lifted it carefully out of the earth.

Before I raised the lid, I glanced at Kristi. She was standing several feet away, ready to run.

"Don't you want to see?" I asked.

"No," she whispered. "It's going to be something awful."

Turning back to the box, I began prying the lid off. Kristi crept closer, and when I finally got it open, she screamed at the sight of its contents.

"It's a dead girl!" she cried.

She startled me so much that I hurled the box into the weeds and backed away from it, terrified.

"I saw it, I saw its face!" Kristi was kneeling in the weeds, her hands over her eyes. "Oh, Ashley, what should we do?"

My heart was thumping and I could hardly breathe, but I forced myself to look at what had fallen from the box. Too small to be a person, it lay in the weeds, face down, its clothing in rags, its hair tangled.

Cautiously I reached out and turned it over. Its china face was pale and smudged with dirt. One eye was half-open and the other was closed, its nose was chipped, but it was still beautiful.

I held it toward Kristi. "It's an old doll," I whispered.

"Are you sure?" Kristi peeked through her fingers like someone watching a horror movie.

I touched the doll's tiny teeth with the tip of my finger and then tried to wipe the dirt from her round cheeks. "Of course I'm sure. Isn't she pretty?"

Finally satisfied we hadn't dug up a dead body, Kristi came closer and stroked the doll's hair. "Can I hold her?"

"Be very careful with her." Reluctantly I handed the doll to Kristi and watched her anxiously. "Don't poke at her teeth or her eyes," I said.

"It's a shame she's so dirty." Kristi pulled the doll's ragged dress up and examined her jointed legs. "Her body's made of leather."

I reached for the doll, but Kristi ducked away. "Let me look at her," she said. "I've never seen one like this."

Although I wanted to snatch it back, I let Kristi examine the doll. I picked up the wooden box. Inside I found a scroll of yellowed paper tied with a faded blue ribbon. On the paper was written:

> *Louisa Perkins, Please forgive me,*
> *I am sorrie.*
> > *Your friend, Carrie.*

I read the message out loud and then swapped the scrap of paper for the doll. Kristi studied the words, her forehead creased.

"It doesn't make sense," she said finally. "Is the doll's name Louisa Perkins?"

I shook my head. "Her name is Anna Maria." I showed Kristi the letters carved on the lid of the box.

"Well, who are Louisa and Carrie then?" Kristi stared at me, obviously puzzled.

I gazed into Anna Maria's one open eye and wished she could talk. "I guess Carrie's the one who buried her," I said slowly, "but I don't know who Louisa Perkins is."

For a moment we were silent, and a breeze sprung up, shaking the Queen Anne's lace and bringing the smell of roses to us. The garden was very quiet, and my voice seemed to hang on the air repeating, "Louisa Perkins, Louisa Perkins." Who was she?

Why was Carrie sorry? And why had she buried the doll?

Suddenly Kristi grabbed my arm. "Look behind you," she whispered. "The white cat's under the bush!"

Chapter 6

Snowball

I STARED AT the cat, and he stared back. His eyes were large and pale green, and his fur was pure white. He looked every bit as real as Oscar, and as he approached me, he began to purr. Timidly I extended a hand and the cat sniffed it slowly. This time he acquainted himself with every finger before he let me stroke his sleek side.

As the cat rubbed himself against me, I glanced at Kristi. Still hiding her face in her hands, she was crouching a few inches away. "Is it gone?" she whimpered.

"He's just an ordinary cat," I told her. "Can't you hear him purring?"

Keeping her eyes squeezed shut, Kristi moved her

hands to cover her ears. "Make it go away, Ashley," she begged. "Make it go away!"

Ignoring her, I let the cat climb into my lap. While he sniffed Anna Maria's hair and clothes, I examined the leather collar he wore around his neck. On a little brass tag was the name *Snowball*. Not very original, I thought, but when I said it aloud, he purred louder and bumped his face against mine.

"Kristi," I said, "stop acting like a baby. He's no ghost. He must belong to someone. He even has a name – Snowball."

Kristi slowly opened her eyes and stared at Snowball. She frowned and shook her head, obviously unconvinced. "Nobody around here has a cat like that, Ashley."

"Maybe he jumped out of a car or something." I smiled at Snowball and he meowed and rubbed against Anna Maria. Then he slipped out of my arms and sniffed the box. He went over every inch of it with his little pink nose, his body tense, his ears pricked. When his nose had told him all it could, he looked at me. For a second I expected him to speak, but he swung his head toward the house instead and crouched beside me, his ears pressed against his skull.

At the same moment, Max started barking. Peering through the jungle of rosebushes and weeds between us and the lawn, I saw Max running toward us with Miss Cooper hobbling behind him.

"Quick, hide Anna Maria!" I thrust the doll into the box and Kristi shoved it deep into the brambles. I was sure Miss Cooper would take her if she saw her. After all, we'd found the doll on her property.

Snowball followed Anna Maria into the shrubbery, but he wasn't fast enough to avoid Max. The dog crashed through the underbrush and chased the cat across the lawn. Snowball ran past Miss Cooper like a white streak and disappeared under the hedge separating her yard from the empty lot.

It would have been smart to stay hidden, but I was worried about Snowball. As I plunged out of the shrubbery, shouting at Max, Miss Cooper waved her cane at me.

"You, girl!" she cried. "Didn't I tell you to stay out of the garden?"

"Call your dog back!" I shouted. "He'll hurt Snowball!"

Miss Cooper stared at me. "That cat doesn't need any help from you or me," she muttered. "The devil takes care of his own!" Her voice quavered, and she clutched her cane so tightly the knuckles on her hands whitened.

Max came back then, and Miss Cooper called him to her side. He dropped to his haunches and growled at me as I edged away slowly, determined not to let the dog know I was scared of him. Suddenly Miss Cooper's hand shot out and caught my arm.

"Where's that Smith girl?" she asked.

As far as I knew, Kristi was still hiding in the garden, but I shook my head and pretended not to know what the old woman was talking about.

"She had better not be in my roses." Miss Cooper let me go and hobbled toward the garden. Prodding the shrubbery with her cane, she called, "You come out of there, girl, or I'll send Max in to get you!"

"Miss Cooper, Ashley, what's the trouble?" Mom was coming down the steps, and Miss Cooper wheeled about to face her.

"You better get some control of this girl," the old woman told Mom. "I already talked to you once today about her. Like I said, I'll have you out of here next week if she doesn't start behaving!"

Without another word, Miss Cooper snapped her fingers at Max and the two of them walked away. Mom stared after her, but she didn't try to stop her. As soon as Miss Cooper's door slammed shut, Mom turned to me.

"Ashley, what's going on?" Mom pushed her hair behind her ears, and I noticed the long silvery threads shining in the dark waves. Ever since Daddy died, I thought, the gray hairs had multiplied along with the tiny lines around her eyes that saddened her face.

Feeling guilty for taking her away from her work, I put my arms around her waist and hugged her.

"I'm sorry, Mom," I whispered. "She's such an old grouch."

"I know, honey," Mom said. "But if she evicts us, where will we find another place? Until I get a job, we have to be very careful with money."

"I'll try not to bother her," I promised, but I knew the very fact that I walked on the floor over her head annoyed Miss Cooper.

"Let's go inside," Mom said. "I made some iced tea."

Although I hated to leave Anna Maria in the garden, I followed Mom toward the house. Miss Cooper was probably watching me from her kitchen window, just waiting to catch me, her finger poised on the telephone dial ready to call the real estate company.

As I started up the steps, I glanced back and saw Kristi run across her yard. I was glad she, at least, had escaped Miss Cooper's anger.

*

That evening while Mom and I were sitting on the porch, I glanced at the garden, darkening now as night approached. Poor Anna Maria was lying alone under the bushes. It wasn't right to leave her there with nothing to protect her. Later, when Mom was asleep, I decided I'd sneak outside and bring Anna Maria into the house where she'd be safe.

"Is that the cat you saw?" Mom asked suddenly.

I peered into the dusk and glimpsed Snowball's white fur as he vanished into the garden. A little shiver ran up and down my arms and lingered at the back of my neck as Miss Cooper's words echoed in my ears. Was Snowball the devil's creature?

Chapter 7

A Midnight Adventure

WHEN I GOT into bed, Oscar was curled up on my pillow waiting for me. He purred happily while I petted him, and when he'd had enough affection, he settled down on the windowsill to watch the night.

Was he waiting for Snowball? Crawling to the foot of my bed, I peered down at the yard. Mom was still typing, and an oblong of light from Miss Cooper's kitchen window slanted across the grass. Fireflies winked and blinked in the shadows, but the garden was nearly invisible in the darkness.

I waited till my eyelids got so heavy I could barely see, but there was no sign of Snowball. Just the crickets chirping, the leaves rustling, and now and then a passing car. Once the kitchen door opened and Max bounded out. I watched him run around the backyard, his dog tags jingling, but he didn't go into the garden and he didn't bark. He just did his business and went back inside.

After the door shut behind Max, the kitchen light went out, and the backyard surrendered itself to the moon. Its full face peered down from high in the sky, brightening the water in Miss Cooper's birdbath, illuminating the clusters of Queen Anne's lace in the garden, casting black shadows everywhere else.

A little later, Mom's typewriter stopped clicking. I listened to her moving around, getting ready for bed.

When everything was still, I looked at my clock radio, glowing green on top of the bureau. It was after twelve. Taking my flashlight, I crept out of my room, shutting Oscar inside to keep him from following me.

I eased the back door open and tiptoed down the steps. They were already cool and damp with dew, and I shivered as a little breeze puffed my nightgown away from my legs. All around me, the night lived its secret life. As I ran across the grass toward the garden, I felt as if a host of creatures watched me from the inky black shadows.

I paused at the end of the lawn and looked back at the house. All the windows were dark, but the moonlight shone full on the white clapboard and sent an intricate shadow from the stairs slanting across the wall. I was sure Oscar was still at his post, and I hoped he was the only one to see me slowly push aside the bushes and creep into the garden.

Brambles snatched at my hair and my nightgown as I made my way slowly toward the goldfish pond. A spider's web brushed my face, frightening me with its clammy touch, but I told myself I wasn't a baby like Kristi. There was nothing in the garden to hurt me. Nothing to scare me.

When I was sure I was invisible from the house, I sent the beam of my flashlight darting through the underbrush, seeking Anna Maria's box. Shadows danced around me and another gust of wind flipped the leaves silver side up. Where had Kristi hidden the doll?

Hearing a faint meow, I turned the flashlight in the sound's direction and saw Snowball crouched beside the box. His eyes reflected the beam of light, and his fur glimmered.

"You found her for me, didn't you?" I whispered as he rubbed against me.

Snowball purred louder when I shone the light into the open box. In its beam, Anna Maria looked pale and worn with age; her face seemed as sad as Mom's.

"You'll be safe now," I told her. "I'll take good care of you and love you and never let you go, Anna Maria."

As I whispered to the doll, Snowball tried to

wedge himself between her and me. Putting his paws on the doll's body, he kneaded her with his claws and meowed like a baby kitten.

"No, Snowball." I pushed him away. "You'll tear her clothes."

Still meowing, the cat backed into the shrubbery, and when I reached for him, sorry I'd hurt his feelings, he edged farther away. I crawled toward him, but he turned and ran out of the garden. Holding Anna Maria tightly, I stumbled after him.

"Snowball," I whispered, keeping a fearful eye on Miss Cooper's windows. "Kitty, kitty, kitty."

Slowly he walked across the grass, watching me over his shoulder as if he were asking me to come with him. When he reached the hedge separating Miss Cooper's yard from the field next door, I stopped.

"Come here, Snowball," I said softly, but he stayed where he was and meowed plaintively.

"I'm not going through that hedge," I told him, "so you'd better come here."

I guess I spoke too loudly because Max started barking from somewhere in the house. Afraid of being caught by Miss Cooper, I turned and ran for the stairs. Up I went as quickly and as quietly as possible. Just as I reached the porch, I saw a light flash out of the open kitchen door below me.

"Who's there?" Miss Cooper yelled. Max bounded

outside barking and ran toward the hedge, and I slipped into our kitchen, still clutching Anna Maria.

Hoping the commotion wouldn't wake Mom, I tiptoed into my room and peeked out the window. Max was circling the yard, sniffing and barking, but I was sure Snowball had his own secret places where Max would never find him.

In a few minutes, Miss Cooper called Max back into the house, and all was quiet again.

I got into bed and Oscar crept to my side. "This is Anna Maria," I told him, holding the doll upright in front of him.

To my surprise, Oscar's back arched and his fur rose. He made a strange growling sound and retreated to the foot of the bed. Hesitating for a moment, he stared at Anna Maria. Then he leaped to the windowsill and refused to come near me or the doll.

"Don't let him hurt your feelings," I whispered to Anna Maria. "He's probably jealous of you."

Anna Maria gazed placidly at me, her mouth slightly open, her tiny teeth showing. She looked as if she were about to take a deep breath and tell me all her secrets.

I smoothed her hair and laid her down beside me. "Who is Carrie?" I whispered. "And why did she bury you?"

But Anna Maria closed her eyes and said nothing.

I closed my eyes, too, happy to have Anna Maria beside me. But just as I was about to fall asleep, I heard it again. Outside in the night, a child was crying.

Frightened, I sat up and looked out the window. Down on the lawn, in full view, I saw Snowball. He was looking up at me, and for the first time I noticed he cast no shadow on the moonlit grass.

Chapter 8

Secrets

WHEN I WOKE UP, the first thing I saw was Anna Maria's pale face beside me on my pillow. Admiring her beauty, I smoothed her hair and straightened her white dress.

Cuddling her close to my chest, I knew I didn't want to share her with anybody. Not Kristi. Not Mom. I wanted to keep her for myself. Quietly slipping out of bed, I went over to my dresser. I laid Anna Maria in the bottom drawer and covered her carefully with my sweaters. No one would find her there, I thought.

While I pulled on clean shorts and a tee shirt, I remembered what I'd seen last night. Had Snowball really cast no shadow? Even in the morning sunlight, I shivered a little thinking about it. I must have been mistaken, I told myself. Moonlight is tricky; it can fool you into imagining all sorts of silly things.

Grabbing a brush and comb, I pulled my hair up into a ponytail and walked down the hall to the kitchen.

"You're up bright and early, Ash," Mom said. "Did you sleep well?"

"I heard that sound again – like somebody crying," I said. "And Max was barking – didn't you hear him?"

"You know me," Mom said. "They could drop an atomic bomb next door and it wouldn't disturb me."

"That's because you stay up so late working," I said. "You should go to bed earlier."

Mom shook her head. "The sooner I finish my dissertation, the sooner I'll get a job," she reminded me.

I chewed my English muffin and watched Mom pour cream into her coffee. "If only Daddy were here," I said without thinking. As soon as the words slipped out, I felt my eyes fill up with tears, and I pressed my hand against my mouth, too late to take back what I'd said.

Mom reached across the table to pat my arm. "I wish he were here, too, Ashley," she said softly. "Don't feel bad for saying you miss him. I miss him too. It's okay to talk about him."

But I couldn't talk about Daddy. Not to Mom, not to anybody. He'd left such a big hole in my life, I knew nothing could ever fill it up. Just saying his name made the hole bigger, so it was better to say nothing.

Pulling away from the comfort Mom was offering me, I went back to my bedroom and took a book from the shelf under the window. I didn't want to see Kristi, not now that Anna Maria lay hidden in my dresser drawer.

*

It wasn't long, though, before I heard Kristi calling me. When I didn't answer, she came to the back door and knocked. Mom let her in and sent her down the hall to my room.

"Ashley, something awful has happened," Kristi said. "Anna Maria's gone!"

I stared at her, trying my best to look surprised. "What do you mean?"

"I went to the garden first thing this morning, and all I found was the empty box." Kristi's eyes glistened with tears, and I struggled to keep myself from feeling sorry for her.

"I thought you weren't ever going there again," I said, reminding her of what she'd told me yesterday.

"I was worried all night about Anna Maria," Kristi explained. "I could hardly sleep for thinking about her lying there by herself in the dark. And I kept hearing that crying and I got to imagining it was her, Anna Maria, crying for me to get her and bring her inside. So the minute I woke up, I went out and looked for her, but she was gone!"

"She must be there," I said, hoping Kristi wouldn't guess I had Anna Maria hidden in a drawer two feet from where she was standing.

"I think the white cat took her," Kristi said sadly. "Or else Max got her and tore her to bits. I heard him outside barking."

Too ashamed to look at Kristi, I just shook my head as if I didn't believe her.

"Come on, Ash, I'll show you." Kristi ran down the hall to the kitchen door, and I followed her reluctantly.

As we slipped through a hole in the hedge at the back of Kristi's yard, I told myself I had every right to keep Anna Maria. Wasn't I the one who opened the box? If I'd listened to Kristi, we would've reburied poor Anna Maria without even seeing her face.

"See?" Kristi dived into the brambles and pulled out the empty box. "All that's left is the note."

I frowned at the little scrap of paper, and, while Kristi was examining the box, I slipped the note into my pocket.

"What should we do?" Kristi stared at me, her eyebrows drawn down over her eyes.

I shrugged and turned away from her to watch a butterfly on a cluster of Queen Anne's lace. It was an orange-and-black monarch, so close I could have touched it with a fingertip.

"You took her, didn't you?" Kristi said suddenly.

I looked at her, feigning innocence. "Why would I do a thing like that?" Unfortunately, my voice came out unnaturally high and I stammered on the words.

"Because you want her for your own!" Kristi hurled the empty box into the bushes.

I drew myself up as tall as I could, glad I was both older and bigger than Kristi. "You were scared to death, remember? You told me to bury the box and you begged me not to open it. You thought Anna Maria was a dead girl!"

Kristi's face got red. "I have just as much right to that doll as you have!" she yelled.

"You do not. This is my yard, not yours!"

"It's Miss Cooper's yard!" Kristi's voice was getting louder and louder.

"Will you shut up?" I hissed. "Miss Cooper and Max are sitting on the front porch. They'll hear you!"

"I don't care if they do!" Kristi shrieked. "You give me that doll, right now, or I'm telling!"

"Be quiet, Kristi!" I wanted to shake her I was so mad. Through the tangle of honeysuckle and shrubbery, I could see Max coming around the corner of the house.

As Max started barking, Kristi scurried away

through the undergrowth, heading for the safety of her backyard. At the same moment, Snowball crept out of the weeds and rubbed against my legs. When I reached for him, he backed away through the brambles, meowing at me, his eyes imploring me to follow him.

Ghost or not, Snowball's fur was soft and his body was as warm as Oscar's. I wanted to pick him up, but before I could catch him, he darted out of the garden and ran across Miss Cooper's lawn.

Afraid Max would get him, I followed Snowball onto the lawn and through a small opening in the hedge that separated Miss Cooper's yard from the field next door. Behind me Max was barking, and I expected to feel his teeth sink into my leg at any moment.

Chapter 9

Louisa

As I stepped out of the hedge on the other side, the light dimmed, and instead of the field, I saw a white frame house in the center of a green lawn. In the sudden dusk, its windows glowed softly, lit from within. The scarlet flowers bordering the porch held the last light of the sun in their petals. The air was cool, fresh, and sweet with the smell of roses. While I stood there staring, I heard a mourning dove begin to coo.

Feeling dizzy, I shut my eyes and backed up against the hedge. Its stiff leaves poked my neck, reassuring me with their scratchiness. Keeping my eyes closed, I wondered if I'd fainted from the heat. I'd read once that people with sunstroke hallucinated. Was that what was wrong with me?

"There's no house here, no flowers," I told myself.

I'd looked over the hedge from my bedroom window, and all I'd ever seen was an empty lot grown high with weeds.

But when I opened my eyes, the house was still there. It was dusk instead of noon, and Snowball was meowing.

Too frightened to move, I looked down at the cat. "What are you?" I asked, remembering Miss Cooper's words about the devil and his own. "Where have you brought me?"

He purred and rubbed against me, warm and soft, his back arched, his tail brushing my legs. Surely he meant me no harm. He was too beautiful to be evil.

As the colors of day faded slowly away, Snowball pricked up his ears. Somewhere in the gray shadows, a child had begun to cry.

Snowball looked at me, and then, his tail waving like a white plume, he disappeared into the shadows on the lawn, leaving me all alone.

Unsure if I were awake or asleep, I was afraid to leave the safety of the hedge. I still didn't know where I was or why Snowball had led me here. I wanted to run back to my own yard, but the child's voice tugged at me. I felt its sorrow, and I had no choice but to follow Snowball.

Like a swimmer venturing deeper into the water, leaving the shore farther and farther behind, I entered the yard a step at a time, pausing after each one to test the current. "Snowball," I whispered. "Where are you?"

Then ahead of me I saw her, a little girl in a white dress, sitting on a stone bench under a dogwood tree. She was holding Snowball on her lap, and her face was hidden by long, golden curls. At her side was a wicker doll carriage as old-fashioned as the clothes the girl wore.

For a moment I stood still, partially hidden by the boxwood bushes lining the path, and watched the girl stroke Snowball's fur. The cat looked at me, his pale eyes expressionless, but the girl didn't see me.

"Where have you been, Snowball?" she whispered. Her voice was low and hoarse, and she was thin and pale.

For an answer, Snowball purred and leapt lightly from the girl's lap. He ran toward me, and the girl looked up and saw me before I could duck away and hide.

Her eyes were huge and darkly shadowed, and her skin was milky white. She gasped and clasped her hands over her chest. "Who are you?" she asked. "Where did you come from?"

For a moment I couldn't speak. Was I staring at a real girl or a ghost? If I answered her, would I be caught in this place forever?

Snowball rubbed against me again, pressuring me to speak, to move, to approach the little girl who sat still, her eyes wide and full of questions, waiting for me to say something.

I closed my eyes again, pressing the lids together so tightly I felt dizzy. If she were there when I opened them, I would know she was real and I would answer her. Aware of my heart beating faster and faster, I slowly allowed myself to look again at the little girl. She had risen to her feet and she looked as puzzled as I felt.

Cautiously I bent down and picked up Snowball. He felt as warm and heavy as Oscar as I walked up to the bench and handed him to her.

"My name is Ashley," I told her. "Your cat brought me here."

The little girl stroked Snowball's soft fur. "You were supposed to bring Carrie," she whispered to the cat. "But she still won't come, will she?"

Lifting her head, the little girl smiled at me. "I've been waiting so long for Carrie, but she never comes. Since you're here, will you stay a while and play with me instead?"

"What's your name?" My heart was still thumping and my knees felt a little quivery, but I had to know who she was.

"My name is Louisa," she said.

"You're Louisa?" I sucked in my breath. "Louisa Perkins?"

She nodded, obviously pleased I knew her name. "Did Carrie tell you about me?"

I shook my head. "I don't know who Carrie is."

Louisa started to speak, but her words turned into a deep, choking cough. Raising a handkerchief to her mouth, she bent her head. Her shoulders shook as the coughing continued.

"You're sick," I said. "You should be in bed."

Louisa shook her head and slowly the coughing stopped. Before she stuffed the handkerchief into her pocket, I saw bright red spots on it.

"Is that blood? Are you coughing up blood?" I stepped back, horrified.

Louisa kept her head down, hiding her face from me. "It's nothing," she said in a low voice.

Frightened, I looked away. Beyond the hedge, I saw the dark shape of Miss Cooper's house against the evening sky, but the steps leading to our apartment were gone and so was our back porch. The tall tree between Kristi's yard and Miss Cooper's wasn't there.

Things were the same and not the same. Like someone in a story, had I followed a white cat into another world? Suddenly afraid I'd never see my mother again, I backed away from Louisa.

"Oh, don't go, please don't go, Ashley." Louisa stood up and clutched my arm. Her hands were icy cold, and her white dress brushed against me as soft as cobwebs. "I'm so lonely. Carrie never plays with me anymore, and I miss Mama and Papa so much."

Snowball circled my legs, meowing, as if he, too, meant to keep me in the garden.

"I'll let you play with my dolls," Louisa said. "Look, here they are." She pointed into the wicker carriage.

Two worn rag dolls sat at each end, facing each other, their heads hanging.

"I used to have another doll," Louisa said. "Her face was china and her hair was the same color as mine. Papa bought her on his last trip to Germany, and I loved her more than anything. Not just because she was beautiful but because Papa gave her to me before he died."

"Your father is dead?" Forgetting to be afraid, I looked into Louisa's eyes and saw the terrible sadness. Sadness like mine, sadness like Mom's.

"He died last fall, and Mama died the year before. Now Aunt Viola takes care of me." Louisa bent over the doll carriage and picked up one of the dolls. "Would you like to play with this one? Her name is Elfrieda."

I took the doll, and Louisa lifted the other from

the carriage. "This is Marguerite," she said. "She's the oldest, that's why she looks so poorly. When I was younger, I fed her jam and tea and stained her face and dress."

Louisa began to cough again. She sank down on the bench, but I stood where I was, clutching the doll. "Have you been to the doctor?" I asked her. "Are you taking medicine?"

"Of course," Louisa said, "but I know I have consumption. Mama and Papa died of it, and so will I. Aunt Viola pretends I'll soon be well and strong, but I'm growing worse, not better. That's why Carrie never comes to play anymore. She's afraid."

I squeezed Elfrieda tighter. "But nobody dies of consumption nowadays," I said.

Louisa stared at me. "You must be a very ignorant girl," she said. "Surely you know better than that."

I bit my lip, and my heart thumped faster and harder against my ribs. "There must be something you can do," I whispered. "A different doctor, a hospital, medicine."

"No," Louisa said. "I heard the doctor talking one day in the parlor with Aunt Viola. He told her my lungs were so weak I'd die before autumn."

While I tried to think of something to say, Louisa bent her head over Marguerite and rocked her gently, crooning a little lullabye.

"Aren't you scared?" I let myself ask the question and then stepped back, horrified by what I'd said.

"Of dying?" Louisa looked up at me. "A little, but I'll be with Mama and Papa, Ashley." Then she smiled at me. "Don't run away like Carrie. Stay with me a while."

She patted the bench beside her, and I sat down next to her. From the carriage, she took out a doll-sized set of china and pretended to make tea for Elfrieda and Marguerite. Although I hadn't played make-believe with dolls for a long time, I joined the game, and as the minutes passed, I almost forgot where I was.

When a voice called from the house, I was so startled I nearly dropped the tiny teacup I was holding to Elfrieda's mouth.

"That's my Aunt Viola," Louisa sighed. "It's time for me to go inside." Taking Elfrieda from me, she laid her and Marguerite in the carriage and gathered up the china.

"Will you give Carrie a message?" Louisa asked me.

"Where does she live?"

"Right there, in that house." Louisa pointed next door at Miss Cooper's house. "You must know her. She's ten years old, just about your size, and she has freckles like you. Her hair's long and brown like yours but she usually has a blue ribbon in it."

I shook my head, terribly confused. "Do you mean Kristi?"

"No." Louisa frowned. "You must find Carrie and you must tell her to bring Anna Maria back. She's had her ever so long. If she knew how much I miss her, she'd give her to me. I know she would."

Aunt Viola called again, louder this time. "Louisa, come inside at once. You know the night air is bad for you."

"I must go," Louisa said. "Please, will you come and play with me again, Ashley?"

"Yes," I whispered, "if I can."

"Just follow Snowball," Louisa said. "He knows the way."

"And I'll bring Anna Maria," I called after her. "I promise I will."

Louisa turned and smiled. "That would make me very happy."

Wanting to tell her more, I tried to follow Louisa down the path, but Snowball tangled himself around my feet and forced me toward the hedge. He let me pause long enough to see Louisa climb the steps toward the tall figure of her aunt waiting by the door. While I watched, Louisa turned and blew me a kiss before the door closed. Then, at Snowball's insistence, I stumbled through the narrow gap into the blinding sunlight of Miss Cooper's backyard.

Chapter 10

Kristi's Revenge

FOR A FEW SECONDS I felt as if I had just stepped out of a dark movie theater into the blazing noontime sun. I could barely see, and I was so dizzy I had to sit down. The world spun, and I clung to the grass, nauseated.

Gradually the trees stopped swaying, and I could look around me without feeling sick. I saw the stairs to our apartment, I saw the tree in Kristi's yard, I saw Mom's car in the driveway – all the familiar things whose presence I'd taken for granted until Snowball led me away from them. I was back, and to my relief nothing was changed.

I took a deep breath and looked behind me at the hedge. Its leaves fluttered in the breeze and from somewhere in its green depth a chorus of locusts droned. Cautiously I stood up and peered through a gap in the branches.

I saw no house, no garden, no Louisa – just a field grown tall with weeds, the same field I saw whenever I looked out my window. Rubbing my eyes hard with my fists, I looked again, half expecting to see the house take shape, but the field kept its secrets. Queen Anne's lace swayed where the roses had grown, black-eyed Susans and day lilies bent their heads where the bench had been. Instead of Louisa, a butterfly hung in the air between me and the elm tree which once sheltered her house.

Had I been dreaming after all? I shook my head. Louisa had been as real as Kristi. I'd felt her hand on my arm, her white dress had brushed against my leg, I'd held Elfrieda in my arms. It had all happened, I was positive.

As a car roared down the street, I forced myself to push through the hedge again. I had to find Louisa, I had to tell her I knew where Anna Maria was. And somehow, like it or not, I had to return the doll to her. She needed her more than I did, more than Kristi did, more than Carrie ever had.

This time, nothing changed when I stepped into the field. The sun shone as brightly as ever, the heat pressed down on me, and the weeds stayed weeds.

I called Louisa's name softly, but there was no answer except the twitter of birds and the rustle of leaves. The sound of my voice seemed to linger in the air, small and sad. I walked farther into the field, pushing my way through waist-high pokeberry bushes, seeking the spot where Louisa's house had stood.

All I found was the foundation, its sides crumbling away. It was almost completely hidden by bushes and clumps of honeysuckle, but it proved a house had stood here once; I hadn't imagined it. Peering into the damp darkness, I called Snowball, but he, too, seemed to have vanished.

Finally, with gnats humming around my head, I gave up my search. I'd have to wait for Snowball, I decided. As Louisa had told me, he knew the way to her world and back again to mine.

Slowly, kicking my way through the weeds, I started toward the street, but before I reached the sidewalk, I saw Miss Cooper and Max walking toward me.

"You," she called to me, "come here this minute."

Although I felt like running in the opposite direction, I knew Miss Cooper would simply complain to Mom again or, worse yet, she'd call up the real estate agent and demand our eviction. Thinking it would be better for me to face her myself, I joined her on the sidewalk.

"I saw you poking around that old foundation. Don't you know it's dangerous to play in places like that?" Miss Cooper bent toward me, her face level with mine. This close, she reminded me of a snapping turtle I'd seen once. Like his, her eyes were small and red rimmed, kind of yellowy and deeply hooded, and her chin vanished in folds of wrinkled skin.

"I can take care of myself," I told her, trying hard not to sound sassy.

"There're snakes in that hole," Miss Cooper informed me. "Copperheads."

"I didn't see any."

"You take my word for it, missy, and stay away from there." She shook her head grimly, taking in my whole appearance. Her eyes lingered on my skinned knees and then moved down to focus on my bare feet.

"Girls today have no manners," she said. "No upbringing. They don't know the meaning of respect. They just run wild. If you were my daughter, I'd never let you out in public looking like you do."

Leaving me too angry to speak, Miss Cooper gave Max's leash a sharp tug and the two of them went off down the street.

Not knowing what else to do, I dragged myself home through the summer heat. As I climbed the steps, I thought I saw Kristi in her treehouse, but when I called to her, she didn't answer. I was sure she was crouching behind the leaves, watching me, still mad about Anna Maria. I wondered what she'd say if I told her where I'd been and what I'd seen.

*

"Where's Kristi today?" Mom asked later while we were having lunch.

"I don't know." To avoid saying more, I took a big bite of my peanut butter and jelly sandwich, but it stuck to my throat and I had to wash it down with lemonade. I wanted to tell Mom about Anna Maria and my fight with Kristi; even more, I wanted to tell her about Snowball and Louisa and the amazing thing I'd done, but I didn't know how to begin or what to say. It was all so strange I could hardly believe it myself.

"You didn't quarrel, did you?" Mom finished her yogurt and buttered a piece of raisin bread while she waited for me to answer.

"She's only seven years old," I said after I'd choked down the last of my sandwich.

"What's that got to do with anything?"

"I'm almost eleven," I reminded Mom. "I don't like playing with babies."

Pushing back my chair, I took my plate and glass to the sink. "Do you want me to wash the dishes so you can get back to your typing?" I asked Mom.

"Are you changing the subject, Ash?" Mom stood

up, too, but as she passed the window she glanced down into the yard.

"There's Kristi now," she said, "talking to Miss Cooper."

I ran to the window. Sure enough, Kristi and Miss Cooper were standing in the driveway under Kristi's treehouse. While I watched, Kristi pointed to the garden and she and Miss Cooper set off across the lawn. As they disappeared into the shrubbery, I felt my knees go weak.

Mom turned to me. "What on earth are they doing?"

I bit my lip hard as they came back into sight. Kristi was still talking, trotting along beside Miss Cooper, but the old woman was ignoring her. In Miss Cooper's hand was Anna Maria's empty box, and she was looking up at me, her face clenched like a wrinkled fist.

Chapter 11

Miss Cooper's Demand

MOM LOOKED AT ME. "Ashley, what have you done now?"

"Nothing," I whispered as I listened to Miss Cooper's feet thump slowly up our stairs.

Mom went to the door and opened it just as Miss Cooper stepped onto the porch.

"That girl," the old woman said to Mom, "took something of mine and I want it back!" She was out of breath from the climb to our apartment, but her eyes bored into me with such anger I drew back frightened.

Mom turned to me. "Ashley?"

"I didn't take anything of hers," I said.

Miss Cooper shoved the empty box under my nose. "Where's my doll?"

"I don't know." I wasn't used to lying, and my voice sounded like someone else's, weak and trembly, almost a whisper.

"You're lying, missy! You stole her and hid her away somewhere, and I want her back." Again Miss Cooper was eye to eye with me, and I felt like a bird facing a snake.

"Miss Cooper," Mom said, "please tell me what you're accusing Ashley of."

The old woman swung her head toward Mom. "There was a doll in this box, a valuable antique doll, and your girl stole it."

"A doll?" Mom sounded confused.

"In the garden," Miss Cooper said. "*My* garden where I told them they had no right to play. But she and that Smith child, they went in there and tore things up, flowers and all, just destroyed everything, and this one stole the doll."

"Ashley, is this true?" Mom's face was pale, and her eyes probed mine.

"We were fixing the garden up," I told Mom, "making a place to play. We didn't pull up anything but weeds." I started crying then, I couldn't help it. If Miss Cooper got her hands on Anna Maria, I'd never be able to return her to Louisa.

Mom put her arm around me, and I pressed my face against her side, ashamed of my tears. I hadn't cried for a long time, not since Daddy first got sick.

"Don't you hide behind your mother!" Miss Cooper's voice rose angrily.

Just then the telephone rang in the living room. "Excuse me," Mom said as she went to answer it.

"Give me what's mine!" Miss Cooper hissed at me.

"She's not yours," I sobbed, "she's Louisa's!"

Miss Cooper stepped backward so fast she almost stumbled over Oscar. "What did you say?" she gasped.

"I said she's Louisa's doll." I stared at the old woman, puzzled. What did she want with a doll anyway? And how did she even know about her? Unless she'd buried her there herself. My hand flew to the old scrap of paper in the pocket of my shorts, but I didn't need to look at it. I knew who had signed the letter.

In the silence, I stared at Miss Cooper. "You're Carrie," I whispered, sure I was right. "You're the one who stole the doll, not me!"

Miss Cooper grabbed for the edge of the table. Her face was white and her mouth sagged open. Trembling, she sank down on a kitchen chair.

At that moment Mom came back into the room. "Are you all right?" she asked the old woman.

Watching Miss Cooper, I tried to see the freckle-faced little girl Louisa had described, but all I could see was the old woman she had become. Nothing of the child Louisa had known remained.

Suddenly Miss Cooper got to her feet. "You get my doll," she said to Mom. "And bring her down to me, or I'll have you out of my house tomorrow."

Refusing to let Mom help her, Miss Cooper opened the back door and began making her way down the steps.

I ran after her but stopped at the edge of the porch. Looking down on her, I could see her scalp through her wispy hair. "I have a message for you," I called softly, hoping Mom wouldn't hear me. "Louisa wants Anna Maria back. You've had her long enough."

Miss Cooper ignored me till she reached the ground. Scowling up at me, she said, "Either you're a lying little hussy or you're the devil's child." Then she vanished around the side of the house.

The screen door opened and shut behind me, and Mom touched my arm. "Maybe you'd better tell me what's going on," she said. "Do you have Miss Cooper's doll?"

As tears welled up in my eyes, I tried to wipe them away with the back of my hand. "It's not hers, Mom," I said. "It belongs to somebody else."

"But you have it?"

I nodded.

"May I see it, please?"

I led Mom back to my room and carefully lifted Anna Maria out from under my sweaters. Wordlessly I laid her in Mom's arms.

"What a lovely doll," Mom said. "Did you really find her buried in the garden?"

"Kristi and I dug her up when we were trying to pull out a thistle. Its roots had gone down deep and it left a big hole in the ground. Kristi saw the corner of the box sticking out of the dirt."

"But why would Miss Cooper have buried her?"

"Because she stole her from somebody else a long time ago."

"How do you know that, Ashley?"

"I just do." I reached for Anna Maria but Mom cradled her against her chest and shook her head.

"I'm sorry, but that's not a good enough answer," she said.

Oscar rubbed against me, purring to get my attention. As I stroked his fur, I let the silence between Mom and me grow until it became impossible to speak. Too often, when I was little, I'd made up stories about fairies and elves and unicorns and sworn they were true. "True make-believe," Mom used to say. If I told her the truth now, she'd never believe me. In fact, more than likely she'd be angry. So, keeping my face hidden, I said nothing.

"You'll have to return the doll to Miss Cooper," Mom said after a while. "You found it on her property."

"No, please don't make me!" Pushing Oscar aside, I threw my arms around Mom, begging her, in every way I knew, to understand.

Mom sat silently on the bed beside me for a few minutes. Finally she said, "Miss Cooper isn't very pleasant and you might not like her very much, but she's old and frail and we're living in her house."

She paused and rubbed my back gently. Outside I could hear Max barking and a lawnmower roaring into life.

"Why don't I take the doll to Miss Cooper?" Mom asked. "Then you won't have to face her."

Taking my silence for a yes, Mom stood up. With my eyes squeezed shut to hold in my tears, I heard her open the back door and walk slowly down the steps. I hoped Kristi was watching. Maybe now that it was too late, she'd be sorry she had told Miss Cooper about Anna Maria.

Chapter 12

Anna Maria Is Lost

I STAYED IN my room reading until Mom called me for dinner.

"Not *The Hobbit* again," she said when I sat down at the table with my book. "This must be the fourth time you've read that."

"I like it," I told her without looking up from the page. Couldn't she tell I was angry with her?

For a few minutes the only sound was the clink of forks against our plates. Then Mom said, "Miss Cooper didn't even thank me for returning the doll. She just snatched it and shut the door in my face."

"What did you expect?" I asked, still not looking at her.

"I know you wanted to keep the doll, Ashley," Mom said, "but surely you're mature enough to realize I had to give it to Miss Cooper."

Instead of looking at Mom, I turned a page, but a big tear plopped down on it, making the words blur. I sniffed and watched the tear flatten out and slowly sink into the paper. Bilbo had just left the Shire to go on his journey with the dwarves, and I wanted to read about his adventures, not talk about Anna Maria.

"This whole business is very strange," Mom said. "I have a feeling you're keeping something from me." She leaned across the table and gently pulled my book away. "Please talk to me."

Again I felt the hated tears rise up and film my eyes. Ignoring the hand Mom laid on mine, I shook my head. There was so much I wanted to tell her, I just didn't know where to begin.

"You've been so brave since Daddy died," Mom continued, "almost too brave. But you're not happy, not the way you were before."

"You're not happy either," I said. "You cry at night – I hear you – and you never laugh."

There was a long silence. The kitchen was slowly darkening and the things around us were losing their outlines and color. It was the time of day I always felt saddest, the gray time when nothing seemed real or solid.

I looked at Mom and she looked at me. Daddy was gone, gone forever from our world, but was there another world where he, like Louisa, still lived his life and made Mom and me laugh at his jokes and stories?

If only Snowball could take me to Daddy, I thought, back to the days before he got sick. But he was Louisa's cat, not Daddy's, and he could only take me to her.

The touch of Mom's hand on my shoulder brought me back to the present, to the table and my uneaten dinner. Even though I couldn't tell her why I was crying, she did her best to comfort me.

*

Long after I went to bed, I lay awake worrying about Louisa. She was counting on me to bring back her doll. Suppose something happened to her before I got Anna Maria away from Miss Cooper? She'd told me she would die before autumn, but I couldn't believe she really would. She was just a little girl. Surely she'd get better.

But I'd thought Daddy would get better, too, and he hadn't. I scowled at the photograph of him I kept on my dresser. In the moonlight, I could see the smile on his face. Turning my head, I tried not to let the terrible anger I felt overwhelm me. It wasn't his fault he died, I told myself. He hadn't done it on purpose; but sometimes I wanted to throw his picture against the wall and scream at him. He'd deserted Mom and me, he'd left us all alone and sad. He'd ruined everything.

When I fell asleep at last, I dreamed about Daddy. He was standing in the yard of our old house in Baltimore. The sun was shining on the grass, and he was tan and healthy and he was laughing.

"Daddy, Daddy," I cried, running toward him. "I thought you were, I thought . . ." But I couldn't finish the sentence, couldn't tell him I thought he was dead.

He hugged me and laughed louder. Then he opened his shirt and showed me his chest. The scar from his operation was gone, his skin was smooth. "You see, Ash? I'm fine. Tell Mommy not to worry. Everything is going to be all right."

I woke up then, and the sunlit lawn was gone and Daddy was gone, and I was lying in the dark in a strange house far from Baltimore, a house Daddy had never seen. And outside in the night Louisa was crying, and there was nothing I could do to comfort her.

Chapter 13

Kristi Comes Too

As soon as I finished breakfast, I ran next door. I was so angry at Kristi, I wasn't sure what I'd do when I saw her. Beat her up maybe. Throw her to Max and let him chew her to bits. Force her to get the doll back.

When I finally found her hiding in her treehouse, Kristi glared at me. "What are you doing on my property?" she asked fiercely. "I didn't invite you up here."

"Why did you tell Miss Cooper about Anna Maria?" I shouted at her. "She has her now, and we'll never see her again. I hope you're satisfied!"

"You shouldn't have taken her," Kristi said. "Anna Maria was supposed to be our secret. We were going to share her!"

"Well, nobody's going to share her now. She's

gone for good, you little baby." I had to clench my fists to keep from slapping her.

"I'm not a baby!" Kristi crouched inches away from me, ready to defend herself. "And you better not hit me either. Brian taught me how to fight, so you watch out what you say to me!"

"I didn't come over here to beat you up," I said. "I just want Anna Maria back!"

"I want her too!" Kristi glared at me, her eyes as hard as little stones. "You're the one who took her and hid her in your house. It serves you right Miss Cooper has her!"

"You don't even know what you've done, do you?" I took a deep breath and decided to tell Kristi everything. She'd be sorry then, wouldn't she?

"It's not for myself I want Anna Maria," I told her. "For your information, she doesn't belong to me or you or Miss Cooper. She belongs to a little girl named Louisa who used to live over there." I waved my hand toward the field, and Kristi stared at the empty lot.

"What are you talking about?" she said scornfully. "There's no house over there. Never has been."

"Just shut up and listen, will you? What I'm going to tell you sounds really weird, but it's true, I swear it." I paused and watched Miss Cooper come outside with Max. She sat down on her porch, opened a book, and started reading. There was no sign of Anna Maria.

"Remember what you said about Snowball being a ghost cat?" I asked.

Kristi sighed. I could tell she didn't want to believe a thing I said. "Yes, but I didn't really mean it," she muttered.

"Well," I said, "you were right."

That got Kristi's attention, and she actually listened to every word I said about Snowball and Louisa. "So you see why you shouldn't have told Miss Cooper we found Anna Maria?" I asked at the end of my story. "I was going to give her back to Louisa and now, thanks to you, I can't."

"Even if you're telling the truth, which I doubt, that old witch won't let us have Anna Maria." Kristi leaned over the edge of the platform and watched Miss Cooper get up and go back into her house.

As the door thunked shut behind the old woman, Snowball appeared in the shade on the edge of the garden. When he approached the tree, I turned to Kristi.

"Suppose Snowball takes us both to Louisa. Will you believe me then?"

Kristi stared at the cat as I started climbing down the ladder. By the time I reached the ground, she was right behind me. "If I go, will you hold my hand?" she asked me.

Although I was still angry, I took her hand. I wanted her to come, to see Louisa herself, to feel really bad about what she'd done.

Together we ran across Miss Cooper's lawn and followed Snowball through the hedge. As before, the sunlight dimmed, and I shivered as I found myself standing once more in the twilight, staring at Louisa's house. It had happened again; I hadn't imagined it. My own world had vanished, and all I could do was hope Snowball would lead us back.

Kristi clung to me, and I could feel her trembling. "I'm scared," she whispered. "Let's go home, Ashley."

"First we have to see Louisa," I said firmly.

Kristi glanced over her shoulder at the hedge behind us. Like me, she saw Miss Cooper's house as it had looked before the porch and stairs to our apartment had been built.

"My tree house is gone," Kristi whimpered. "There's no tree at all, and it's getting dark. Are you sure my mother's there?"

"I've done this before," I told her.

"Why is it so dark? I can see the moon."

"Time is different here," I said, but I wondered myself why it was darker than it had been yesterday.

"I'm cold." Kristi's hand sought mine again as Snowball brushed against us. "Can't we go home now? I don't like this place."

"You have to meet Louisa." I gripped her hand tightly to keep her from trying to bolt back through the hedge.

"I'm afraid of ghosts." Kristi was close to tears.

"Louisa's not a ghost," I said. "When we hear her crying at night in our world, she's a ghost, I think. But here in her world we're the ghosts, not Louisa."

"You're real," Kristi insisted, "and so am I. I can feel you and you can feel me. Besides you have to be dead to be a ghost, and we're not dead."

Snowball meowed then and circled our legs. I picked him up and handed him to Kristi. "He's real, isn't he?"

"He *feels* real," she said, but she put Snowball down quickly. He meowed again and nudged us toward the path.

"Come on," I said. "He wants to take us to Louisa."

"You won't tell her I gave Anna Maria to Miss Cooper, will you?" Kristi asked, still hanging back.

I shook my head and followed Snowball down the shadowy path. Reluctantly, Kristi stumbled along behind me. I knew she was still scared, but I wasn't sorry for her. If she hadn't been such a tattletale, I'd have Anna Maria in my arms right now. Instead, I was returning to Louisa empty handed, and Carrie was once again in possession of the doll.

Chapter 14

Please Give Her Back

RELUCTANTLY, KRISTI let me lead her down the path to the bench under the dogwood tree. When Louisa saw us coming, she stood up slowly.

"Who have you brought with you?" She peered into the shadows behind me. "Is it Carrie?"

"No, it's my neighbor, Kristi." I beckoned to Kristi, but she hung back, her eyes fixed on Louisa as if she expected her to change into something hideous at any moment.

Louisa smiled and extended a small hand, but Kristi wouldn't take it. I knew she was as scared as I'd been the first time I met Louisa.

"You needn't be afraid," Louisa said to her.

"I'm not." Kristi frowned and folded her arms tightly across her chest, refusing to come close enough for Louisa to touch her.

Louisa turned to me. "Did you find Carrie?"

I nodded. What would Louisa think if she could see the mean old woman Carrie had grown into? "But she wouldn't give me Anna Maria."

Louisa sighed. "I didn't think she really would. No matter what Snowball and I do, she won't part with my doll."

"Do you ever see Carrie?" I asked.

"Sometimes." Louisa gazed across the hedge at my house. "There she is right now." She pointed at my bedroom window. "I often see her watching me."

With shivers running up my neck, I turned and saw a girl standing at my window. Her hair was long and dark, but she had her back to the light, making it impossible for me to see her face. When she realized we'd noticed her, she stepped away from the window and closed the curtains.

It made goose bumps rise all over me to think I was looking at my own bedroom, not as it was now, but as it used to be. How could a house exist in two different times at once? If Carrie was in my room, where was Mom? Anxiously, I turned back to Louisa, but she was rocking her doll carriage and humming.

"Would you like to play tea party again?" she asked me. "I brought three dolls today, just in case Carrie came, so Kristi can have Beulah."

Reaching into the carriage, Louisa pulled out a china doll with painted hair and handed her to Kristi. She gave me Elfrieda again and kept Marguerite for herself.

Silently Kristi watched Louisa pour imaginary tea into three tiny cups. In the few days I'd known her, she'd never been so quiet, and I wondered what she was thinking about.

As we pretended to sip our tea, Kristi finally spoke. "Why did Carrie take your doll?" Her face was screwed into a terrible scowl. If she had the chance, I was sure she'd beat up Carrie for making Louisa so unhappy.

Louisa glanced up at my bedroom window as if she expected Carrie to reappear. "Well, you see, Carrie's father never let her have a doll of her own," she said. "He thinks toys encourage idleness." She gave Marguerite a little pat on the head.

"Whenever Carrie came to see me," Louisa went on, "I let her play with Anna Maria because she loved her best. A few days ago, I left Anna Maria in the garden while I ate dinner. When I went outside to get her, I saw Carrie running through the hedge with her. I called and called, but she never came back."

As Louisa's eyes filled with tears, Kristi and I looked at each other. How could Miss Cooper have changed so little? Even now she was as mean and rotten as she'd been when she was a kid.

"We'll get her for you," I told Louisa. "I promise."

Louisa began to cough again, harder this time. "Maybe you should go inside," I told her, frightened by the way her body shook. She was so thin and small and fragile.

"Yes," she said, letting me lead her toward her house. "I'm not supposed to stay outside, but I wanted to be here if you came back to play."

As we walked up the path, I saw Aunt Viola hurrying toward us. To my surprise, she brushed past Kristi and me without seeing us and picked up Louisa as if she weighed no more than Anna Maria. "I thought you were in your room," she said as she carried her up the porch steps.

"My doll carriage," Louisa gasped between coughs. "I left it in the garden."

"I'll bring it in later, after you're in bed." Aunt Viola opened the door, and Kristi and I watched her carry Louisa into the house. Then the door shut, and they were gone.

Alone in the dusk, Kristi and I stared at each other. "Why didn't Aunt Viola see us?" Kristi asked.

"I told you before," I said. "We're the ghosts here."

"But Louisa sees us," Kristi said.

"Maybe it's because Snowball brings us to her." I

looked down at the cat, and he looked at me. Then he walked away toward the hedge. By the light of the moon, I saw his shadow, but when I looked at Kristi, I realized she had no shadow and neither did I.

"Come on, Kristi," I said. "It's time to go back." Taking her hand, I followed Snowball through the hedge.

*

As we stumbled into my yard, the world spun like a carousel. With the sun in my eyes almost blinding me, I heard Mom's typewriter, Max barking, a motorcycle sweeping past, and Mrs. Smith's vacuum cleaner. The steps to our apartment cast a sharp shadow on the side of the house, and the leaves rustled in Kristi's tree.

Feeling a little weak and wobbly, I sank down on the grass beside Kristi.

"Well?" I asked her. "Do you believe me now?"

For a few seconds Kristi just sat there. She was breathing fast, and she was almost as pale as Louisa. "Oh, Ashley," she whispered, "it was all true what you said. I didn't think it would be."

Then, turning her head, Kristi looked back through the hedge. "It's just a field again," she said.

I nodded. "See the big thicket of pokeberries under the elm tree? That's where the house used to be. The foundation's still there."

"I wonder what happened to the house. And to Louisa." Kristi stared at me. "She's sick, isn't she?"

"She told me she has consumption."

"Is that a bad disease? Is it contagious?"

"It was then," I said, "when Louisa was little."

"But there's a cure, right?"

"Now there is."

But back in those days?" Kristi asked. "People didn't die of . . . consumption, did they?"

"Don't worry about it, Kristi," I said. "What we have to do is get Anna Maria away from Miss Cooper."

Kristi sighed and hid her face in her hands. "I wish I hadn't told. I'd give anything to go back to yesterday and make it different."

"It's too late to change it now." I stood up and brushed the dirt off the seat of my shorts. "But maybe we can try."

"Where are you going?" Kristi asked.

"To see Miss Cooper."

"It won't do any good. You'll just get in trouble again," Kristi said, but I didn't pay any attention to her. I was still afraid Miss Cooper might evict Mom and me, but I had to get Anna Maria. I'd keep my promise to Louisa no matter what happened.

Summoning all the courage I had, I marched around the corner of the house and found Miss

Cooper sitting on her front porch, reading the news-paper.

When she saw Kristi and me, she frowned. Grabbing her cane, she levered herself out of her rocking chair.

"You girls get out of here," she said. "You've got no business in this part of the yard."

Kristi started edging away toward the safety of her tree house, but I stood my ground. "Miss Cooper," I said, "please give Anna Maria back to me. I have to have her."

Miss Cooper clutched her cane tightly, and for a few seconds we stood still, eye to eye. Finally she swallowed hard and said, "Yesterday you spoke a lot of nonsense about Louisa." Her voice trembled. "How did you know her name?"

"There was a note in the box you buried. It said, 'Louisa Perkins, please forgive me, I am sorry. Your friend Carrie.'" I held my breath and waited for Miss Cooper to say something. When she didn't, I added, "That's how I know you're Carrie."

"Louisa," she said slowly and her mouth worked around the name as if she hadn't spoken it for a very long time. "Yes, I forgot about the note."

Turning away from me, Miss Cooper gazed across her lawn at the field where Louisa's house had once stood.

"Louisa Perkins," the old woman murmured as if she'd forgotten my existence. "She lived next door, but the house is gone now. It burned down about twenty years ago."

"What happened to Louisa?" I asked.

"Oh," Miss Cooper said, "she died when she was eight or nine."

The words fell from her lips like stones, and it took me a second or two to realize what she'd said. I clutched Kristi's arm, but we didn't look at each other. We just stood there on the lawn while the birds sang around us as if nothing had happened.

Miss Cooper picked up her newspaper and fanned herself with it. "Children died all the time in those days," she muttered.

I stared at Miss Cooper's wrinkled face and red-rimmed eyes. Here she was, an old woman, talking about Louisa's short life as if it hadn't mattered at all. Didn't she feel bad about living so much longer?

Then Kristi's voice cut through the hot summer air. "Louisa still wants her doll," she said, "and you better give it to her!"

The old woman looked at us then. "Go on home," she said, her voice rising, "both of you."

She yanked open the door, but before she went into the house, she added, "I don't know what you're up to, but don't come pestering me again about that doll!"

I ran up the porch steps after her and rapped on the long window beside the closed door. "Give me the doll," I cried. "She doesn't belong to you!"

The house was silent. Pressing my face against the glass, I tried to see inside, but the lace curtain stretched over the window blocked my view.

Angrily I pushed the doorbell and let it ring till it sounded like someone screaming. "Give me Anna Maria!" I yelled. "Give her to me!"

I kicked the door hard, and then, frightened, I turned and ran. With Kristi behind me, I scrambled up the ladder to the tree house.

Chapter 15

How Can We Save Louisa?

"THAT OLD WITCH! I hate her!" Kristi cried. Then she buried her face in her hands and wept. "Why did Louisa have to die?" she sobbed. "Why couldn't she have gotten well?"

"If anybody had to die," I said, "it should have been Miss Cooper, not Louisa."

It was a terrible thing to say, but it was true. The world was so unfair when it came to dying. The best people, the ones you loved the most, died and other people, mean and nasty, lived and went right on being mean and nasty all their lives. Louisa and Daddy – why them and not Miss Cooper?

Fighting back tears, I watched a butterfly come to rest on a hollyhock below me. It fanned its wings, and the sun shone right through them, making them glow. Then a breeze swayed the flower, and the butterfly drifted away.

"If we could give Anna Maria back to Louisa," I said, "maybe she wouldn't die. Maybe we could change what happened."

Kristi's face lit up with hope. "Do you mean we could save her life?"

"Suppose she's getting weaker because she's so sad about losing her doll? If we made her happy, she'd get stronger and maybe she'd get well."

Kristi nodded, but then she frowned again. "We still don't have Anna Maria," she reminded me.

"We'll get her somehow," I said, "even if we have to sneak in Miss Cooper's house and steal her."

When Brian bellowed for Kristi, I scrambled down from the tree house and slowly climbed the steps to our apartment.

Mom was waiting for me on the porch. "Miss Cooper has complained again," she said wearily. "She told me you were rude to her. You rang her bell and banged on the door and then ran into Kristi's yard and hid. Is this true, Ashley?"

I stared down at my bare feet, too ashamed to look Mom in the eye. Without meaning to, I'd upset her and interrupted her work again. Why was I always making her unhappy?

In the growing silence, Mom sighed. "Are you still angry about the doll?"

"She doesn't belong to Miss Cooper!" I stopped and bit my lip. How could I make Mom understand?

Thinking carefully, I asked, "Do you believe in ghosts?"

Mom looked puzzled. "What do ghosts have to do with Miss Cooper and the doll?"

"Just tell me," I said. "Do you believe in them?"

"Sometimes," Mom said. "Especially after your father died. There were mornings when I woke up, sure he was sleeping beside me; times I'd walk into a room positive he'd just left — I'd even smell his pipe smoke, hear his footsteps, catch glimpses of him on crowded streets." Her voice trailed off and she slid her arm around me, hugging me close.

As she held me tightly, I was afraid to look at Mom. I knew how hard she tried to hide her feelings from me, to be brave.

"Did you ever think, though," I asked her, "that maybe he still exists in another time and you could go back to the years before he died and see him again?"

"Oh, Ashley, it was my own memories of Fred, not his actual presence, that haunted me." Mom sighed. She had said all she was going to say on the subject. And she had heard all she wanted to hear.

For a while we sat together, side by side but a million miles apart. If only I could tell her how angry I felt at Daddy for making us so sad, but I was sure she wouldn't understand.

*

That night, I woke up after midnight. Oscar was prowling back and forth on the windowsill, his tail twitching, and Max was barking.

"What's out there?" Miss Cooper cried. "Go get it, Max."

Pressing my face against the screen, I saw Snowball standing in a square of light shining from Miss Cooper's kitchen window. Then Miss Cooper's door opened, and Max charged outside. Snowball stood his ground, and to my surprise, Max retreated while Miss Cooper called, "Shoo, shoo, get away from here!"

While I watched, Snowball stalked toward the house. Like a cat in slow motion, he moved one paw ahead, then another. His bushy tail stood straight up and his fur puffed out, making him look twice his normal size. Even though I knew he meant me no harm, he frightened me.

"Go away!" Miss Cooper begged. "Go back where you belong!"

Her door slammed, and the kitchen light went out. Although the lawn was swallowed up in shadows, I could see Snowball's white fur glimmering. As my eyes grew accustomed to the darkness, I watched him pace back and forth, gazing up at the house. It wasn't me he was looking at this time, and when I called his name he didn't respond.

Twitching his tail, Snowball began to meow.

Gradually he worked himself up into full cry and yowled until he woke Mom.

Joining me at my window, she asked, "is that the cat you were talking about?"

"Isn't he beautiful?"

"Frankly," Mom said, as Snowball continued yowling, "beautiful isn't the first word that comes to my mind when a cat wakes me up at one A.M."

Shoving the screen up, Mom stuck her head out. "Shush!" she yelled at Snowball, "Scat!"

The cat looked up at Mom and me just as Miss Cooper hurled a bucket of water out the back door. He spun about and hissed, then turned and ran across the lawn. While we watched, he darted under the hedge and disappeared into Louisa's yard.

"Old witch," I muttered as Miss Cooper's door slammed.

"Oh, Ashley," Mom sighed. Her hand lingered on my hair, smoothing it as it tumbled down my back. "If she hadn't done it, I'd have thrown the water myself. I need my sleep, and so do you."

She kissed me good night, and I crawled back under my covers, too tired to worry about Louisa. "Don't cry any more tonight," I whispered to her. "Please don't cry. I'll get the doll, I promise."

Chapter 16

Talking to Miss Cooper

WHILE I WAS eating breakfast the next morning, Kristi came thumping up the steps and barged into the kitchen. Taking a seat, she helped herself to a slice of bread and spread a thick layer of jam on it. "Did you hear Snowball last night?" she asked.

"I think he's mad because Miss Cooper won't give Anna Maria to us," I said. "That's why he was yowling at her."

"Miss Cooper must be scared," Kristi said.

"Maybe we should try talking to her again," I said. "She might give us Anna Maria just to get rid of Snowball."

Kristi wiped the back of her hand across her mouth, smearing blueberry jam across her cheek.

"Not me," she said, "I'm never speaking to that mean old woman again."

"We have to get Anna Maria," I reminded her.

While I rinsed my breakfast dishes, I watched Kristi help herself to another slice of bread and jam. She was acting very nonchalant, but I knew she was trying hard to think of some reason not to visit Miss Cooper.

When the kitchen was clean, I opened the back door and started down the steps. Kristi pattered behind me, mumbling to herself.

"You don't have to come with me if you don't want to," I told her. "You can hide in your old tree house like a baby and spy on us."

Kristi glared at me. "Just because I'm younger than you doesn't make me a baby," she said.

While Kristi hesitated, Miss Cooper suddenly appeared in person. Leaning heavily on her cane, she confronted us in the driveway. She looked fiercer than usual, and I backed away from her so fast I stepped right on Kristi's bare toes.

"That white cat," she said abruptly. "You girls put him in my yard last night, didn't you? You were trying to scare me."

"You know who that cat is and where he comes from," I said. I was feeling pretty brave, but my voice sounded shaky. "He's here to get Louisa's doll, and you better give it back before it's too late!"

Miss Cooper gripped her cane tighter and backed away from me. "It's already too late," she said. "Louisa's been dead since 1912. Nothing can change that."

She paused a moment, breathing heavily. "If you don't believe me, go to Cypress Grove Cemetery and see for yourself, missy. Just look for the pink angel her aunt put up for her!"

Kristi looked at me, her eyes full of tears, and I glared at Miss Cooper. "How could you be so mean?" I asked. "Louisa was an orphan, and she was sick. You must have known she was going to die, but you took Anna Maria anyway."

"You had no business digging that doll up!" Miss Cooper snapped at me.

"And you had no business burying her!"

Miss Cooper looked from me to Kristi, her mouth pursing and unpursing. "I just borrowed the doll," she said at last and lifted her chin, daring us to contradict her. "I meant to give her back, but that aunt of hers wouldn't let me in the house. She said Louisa was too sick for company; she said to come back when she was feeling better. I didn't think Louisa was going to die. What does a child know of death?"

"Why didn't you just give Anna Maria to Aunt Viola?" I asked.

Miss Cooper turned her head away, her eyes seeking Louisa's yard. "That woman didn't like me. Nobody did. I was always in trouble. Do you know what Papa would have done if he'd known I'd taken the doll?"

The old woman stared at me, and I shrugged and looked down at my bare feet. I was starting to feel sorry for her, and I didn't want to. Not when she'd been so mean to Louisa.

"He'd have beaten me with his belt," Miss Cooper said, "and then he'd have locked me in the coal cellar and left me there in the dark till he was sure I'd repented."

"Is that why you buried her?" I asked. "So no one would know you took her?"

Miss Cooper nodded. "When they told me Louisa was dead, it seemed the right thing to do. I sneaked out of the house late at night and buried her under Papa's best rosebush. I knew nobody would dare dig near its roots."

She paused a few seconds and then added softly, "I even said the right words, the very ones I heard at Louisa's funeral."

Miss Cooper rummaged about in her pocket and pulled out a wrinkled handkerchief. She blew her nose carefully. "Don't you think I haven't felt bad about it all these years?" she said. "You're too young to know, but the things you do when you're a child stay with you all your life."

"But you can change it now," Kristi said. "You can give Anna Maria to Louisa."

"How can I do that?" Miss Cooper peered at Kristi as if she thought she was crazy. "Louisa's been dead over seventy years. Time doesn't run backward, you know, and things that have been done can't be undone, no matter how hard you wish."

"But Snowball can take us through the hedge to Louisa's garden," I said. "The house is there, and she's there, and so is Aunt Viola. We've seen Louisa and talked to her, that's how we know how much she wants Anna Maria."

"Why are you telling me lies?" Miss Cooper's voice rose and quavered as she leaned toward me. "You are a wicked child."

"I'm not lying!" I was getting angry. "Just give us Anna Maria so we can take her to Louisa before she dies."

Kristi began crying. "Don't you see?" she said to Miss Cooper. "If she gets the doll back, maybe she won't die. We want to save Louisa's life."

I don't know what would have happened if Snowball hadn't come walking across the grass at that moment. Miss Cooper saw him first. "Louisa's cat," she hissed. "Get him away, get him away!"

Picking Snowball up, I caressed his white fur. "He won't leave till you give Anna Maria back," I said. "Won't you please get her? Please!"

The three of us stood facing each other like children frozen in a game of statues. At last Miss Cooper said, "The world's full of white cats. They all look just the same." Her voice was shaking and the hand clutching her cane trembled.

"But they have shadows, right?" While she watched, I set Snowball down on the grass. "All except this one."

Miss Cooper, Kristi, and I looked at the ground at Snowball's feet. His fur shone in the sunlight, his pink nose glistened with health, his big green eyes stared up into ours, but no shadow anchored him to the earth. Meowing softly, he took a few steps toward Miss Cooper and she backed away.

"I knew it all along," the old woman whispered, more to herself than to us. "But I didn't know what they wanted. I told myself they were just tormenting me because I didn't go to see her before she died."

Miss Cooper paused and Snowball rubbed against her legs, purring. She flinched a little, but she didn't move away. Slowly she bent down and ran a hand lightly over his fur. "You feel so real," she said.

Then she straightened up and looked at me. "You say it's the doll. If Louisa gets her back she'll rest quiet and leave me be?"

I nodded, and the old woman sighed. "All right," she murmured. "All right."

Letting out my breath in a long, slow sigh of relief, I watched Miss Cooper hobble around the side of her house and climb her steps. Kristi clutched my arm, and Snowball purred as he watched the house, too, waiting for Miss Cooper to come back with Anna Maria.

Chapter 17

Louisa and Carrie

AFTER WHAT SEEMED like a very long time, Miss Cooper opened her front door and walked slowly toward us. She was carrying Anna Maria as if she were a real baby, and I noticed she'd washed the doll's face and clothes and curled her hair. Except for the chip on her nose, Anna Maria looked almost as good as new.

When I reached for the doll, though, Miss Cooper shook her head. "No," she said, "I'm going with you. If there's any truth in this, I want to see it for myself."

"But Louisa won't know who you are," I said. "She thinks you're still a little girl."

Miss Cooper frowned and stuck her lip out as if she were Kristi's age. "If you want the doll returned, you have to let me do it."

I could tell by the expression on Kristi's face that she didn't want Miss Cooper to come, but to me it made sense. Since she had taken Anna Maria, it seemed right for her to give her back to Louisa.

"Maybe it won't work if she comes," Kristi said to me.

"Maybe it won't work if *you* come." Miss Cooper clutched Anna Maria and scowled at Kristi.

While the two of them glared at each other, Snowball brushed against Miss Cooper and meowed. Forgetting everything else, the three of us followed him around the house and across the backyard. As we approached the gap in the hedge, I looked up at our apartment, hoping Mom wouldn't see us parading across the lawn. She was nowhere in sight, but I could hear the clatter of her typewriter.

"He's waiting for us." Kristi tugged at my arm and pulled me toward Snowball. The cat was standing by the hedge. His green eyes were huge as he watched Miss Cooper walk slowly toward him and stop a few feet away.

"Come on," I took the old woman's arm and tried to pull her toward Louisa's yard.

"I'm afraid." Miss Cooper resisted me. In the hot sunlight, she looked as old and fragile as the doll she held in her arms. "What will happen to me if I go with you?"

Kristi and I looked at each other. "Nothing," I said, but how did I know?

"What's Louisa like?" Miss Cooper asked. "Is she a ghost? A spirit?"

"She's just as real as I am," I said. "She's thin and small and her hair is long and golden, the color of honey."

Miss Cooper's mouth twitched, but she didn't say anything. Lowering her head, she caressed Anna Maria's curls. "I fixed her up the best I could," she said, "but I couldn't do anything about her nose. I hope Louisa won't be mad about it." Miss Cooper looked at me. "Do you think she'll forgive me for treating her so badly?"

From what I knew of Louisa, I was sure she wouldn't bear anyone a grudge. Gently, I led Miss Cooper toward the hedge, and the three of us followed Snowball into the dusky world on the other side.

*

The first thing I noticed was the darkness. It wasn't twilight this time but full night. The moon shone high overhead, and Snowball's fur shimmered as he ran through patches of shadow toward Louisa's house. The air was cool against my skin and a breeze made me shiver.

Kristi grabbed me. "She's gone," she whispered. "She didn't come after all."

"Miss Cooper?" I looked behind me into the dense shadows near the hedge. The leaves stirred and rustled, and, as Kristi and I watched, a little girl appeared. She was shorter than I was, and her long straight hair tumbled around her thin face. In her arms was Anna Maria.

While Kristi and I stood staring, the girl gazed at the house, her eyes scanning the upper story. One light shone from a window. In the silence, I heard her draw in her breath.

Clutching Anna Maria, Carrie Cooper walked right past Kristi and me. Without looking at us, she slowly climbed the back steps and paused at the door where Snowball sat waiting. Cautiously she turned the knob and slipped inside with Kristi and me behind her.

We followed Carrie through an old-fashioned kitchen, down a dark hall, and up a flight of carpeted steps. Scarcely daring to breathe, Kristi and I watched her stop in front of a closed bedroom door. A crack of light shone under it, and Carrie pressed her ear against the wood. Hearing nothing, she opened the door quietly and peered into the room.

Although Kristi and I tried to go with Carrie, Snowball stopped us on the threshold and forced us to stay in the shadows like an audience in a darkened theater watching a play unfold upon a stage.

The room was lit softly by a heavily shaded lamp

beside an old oak bed. In a chair next to the bed sat Aunt Viola, fast asleep. In the bed, her head propped up on a lacy pillow, was Louisa. The lamplight gleamed on her hair, turning her curls to gold, but her eyes were closed and deeply shadowed. Her face was ashy white and her thin hands clutched the covers.

While we watched, Carrie approached the bed, holding Anna Maria like an offering. In the light from the lamp, I could see her sharp face and small, pointed chin, her dark eyes, and the frown creasing her forehead.

As Carrie bent over the bed, Louisa opened her eyes. "Carrie," she whispered. "Is it really you?"

"I brought her back." Carrie laid Anna Maria in Louisa's arms. "I just wanted to borrow her for a little while. I didn't mean to keep her so long." Carrie ran a finger lightly over the doll's hair, but her eyes were fixed on Louisa's pale face.

Louisa smiled. "It's all right," she said, hugging the doll. "You knew how much I needed her, so you brought her."

"I would have come sooner," Carrie said, "but your aunt wouldn't let me in the house." She stole a glance at Aunt Viola who sighed without opening her eyes.

"She tries hard to do what's best for me," Louisa

said, "but she makes mistakes sometimes."

"Are you sure you forgive me?" Carrie came closer to Louisa, and I could hear the tears in her voice.

Louisa reached out and grasped Carrie's hand. "You're my best friend, Carrie. Nothing can ever change that."

Holding Anna Maria tightly, Louisa lay back on her pillow and smiled at Carrie. For a moment her eyes sought mine and Kristi's, but when I tried to approach the bed, Snowball pressed against me, keeping me in the hall.

"Don't leave me, Louisa," Carrie said. "Get well, and I'll be a better friend, you'll see. I'll never tease you or take your things. I promise."

Louisa turned her head and coughed. When she looked at Carrie again, her face was paler. "I'm very tired now," she whispered. "Perhaps you'd better leave. If Aunt Viola awakes and finds you here, she'll be cross."

But Carrie lingered. She smoothed the pillow under Louisa's head and brushed her curls lightly with one hand. "You have Anna Maria now," she said. "She'll make you get well, I know she will."

But Louisa shook her head. "Soon I'll be with Mama and Papa. I heard Doctor McCoy tell Aunt Viola when he thought I was sleeping."

Carrie stared at Louisa, but the little girl's eyes

were already closing. Bending down, she kissed Louisa's cheek. "I'll always be your friend, I promise," Carrie said. "And when you're well, we'll have tea parties in the garden again and you can read to me from your fairy tale book."

Louisa lay still, her eyes closed, a little smile curving her lips. Once more Carrie touched the doll, and then without looking back she ran from the room.

Chapter 18

A Visit to Cypress Grove

THE MOONLIGHT silvered the yard as Snowball led
Kristi and me out of the house. When I looked up at
Louisa's bedroom window, I saw Aunt Viola peering
out into the garden, but she didn't notice me. She
was looking at the hedge, which was swaying as if
someone had run through the gap ahead of us.

"Where's Carrie?" Kristi asked me. "We can't leave
her here."

"She must have gone home without us," I said.

"Let's go." Kristi pushed past me, but I lingered a
moment, watching Louisa's window. Aunt Viola was
gone, but the light still glowed softly.

"Goodbye, Louisa," I whispered, knowing as I
spoke that I would never see her again. She had sent
Snowball to me for the last time, and she was sleeping now with Anna Maria in her arms.

"Come on, Ashley." Kristi pulled my arm. "It's scary here in the dark, and I'm cold."

Ignoring her, I stooped down and stroked Snowball's fur as he rubbed against my legs and purred. "I won't see you again either," I told him.

Tears filled my eyes as he slipped away from me and ran up the steps. Leaping to the sill of an open window, he crawled into the house. I waited and in a few seconds I saw him looking down at me from Louisa's room. Then he was gone and Kristi was pulling me through the hedge.

*

As we stumbled out of the shrubbery and into the afternoon's hot sunlight, we almost tripped over Miss Cooper. As old and wrinkled as ever, she was sitting on the grass in her own yard. When she saw Kristi and me, she said, "It was all true what you told me, all true."

"You gave Anna Maria back to Louisa," I said, "just like you promised."

"Yes," Miss Cooper said, "I did, didn't I?"

"And she forgave you," I added.

Miss Cooper smiled then and her wrinkles shifted and reshifted, forming new patterns. "She died peaceful," she said. "She died my friend."

Stunned, I watched Miss Cooper struggle to her feet. "She couldn't have died," I said. "She couldn't have."

Miss Cooper glanced at me and shook her head. "She died on this very day in 1912. I told you that." Then she hobbled away, leaving Kristi and me standing in the hot sunshine staring after her, too dumbstruck to speak.

"Come on." I grabbed Kristi's arm and started running. Despite the heat, we raced across the lawn and down Homewood Avenue toward Lindale Street.

"Where are we going?" Kristi cried.

"To Cypress Grove," I shouted. "It can't be true, Louisa can't be dead, not after all we did."

By the time we'd run the five blocks to the cemetery, we were panting and soaked with sweat. At the iron gates, I paused a moment, almost afraid to enter the still, green landscape ahead of me.

"You said she wouldn't die if she got her doll back," Kristi said. Her voice was so sharp with accusation you'd think I'd deliberately betrayed her.

Ignoring Kristi, I walked slowly down a gravel roadway. Unlike the memorial park where Daddy was buried with only a brass plate to mark his grave, Cypress Grove was an old cemetery, and you couldn't mistake it for anything but what it was. Many of the stones had fallen over and lay half-buried in the grass. The inscriptions were hard to make out, partly because the writing was old-fashioned and partly because the words had been almost worn away by years of rain and snow.

"If we don't find her grave, then she didn't die," I told Kristi, but even as I spoke I saw the pink stone angel Miss Cooper had told us about. It was standing in the shade of a holly tree, somberly regarding the ivy curling around its base.

It was a hot, dry July day, and leaves from the holly tree littered the ground. As we stepped into its shade, the leaves crunched under our bare feet, cutting our skin with their sharp edges. Sunlight and shadows mottled the little angel. Slowly I made out the letters carved into the stone:

LOUISA ANN PERKINS
BELOVED DAUGHTER OF ROBERT ALAN PERKINS
AND
ADELAIDE JOHNSON PERKINS
JANUARY II, 1903 – JULY 17, 1912
MAY SHE REST IN PEACE
WITH THE ANGELS OF THE LORD

"She died. Louisa died," Kristi whispered.

I grabbed Kristi's hand and squeezed hard. Louisa was as real to me as Kristi, and my eyes filled with tears as I remembered the way she'd hugged Anna Maria and then fallen asleep. We'd tried so hard, Kristi and I and even Miss Cooper, but we hadn't kept Louisa from dying any more than Mom and I had kept Daddy from dying.

We'd failed, and the same anger I'd felt at Daddy redirected itself toward Louisa. Just like him, she'd deserted me. I'd never see her again; I'd never see him again. How could they just turn their backs and leave me?

Sinking to the ground beside Louisa's grave, I cried so hard my chest ached. All my tears for Daddy, the ones I'd held back so long, poured out of me. "How could you do it?" I sobbed. "How could you go?"

Kristi patted my shoulder and whispered something, but it didn't comfort me. It was Daddy I wanted. No one else would do.

Chapter 19

❖————✦❀✦————❖

Flowers for Louisa

I DON'T KNOW how long I cried, but when I finally stopped, I saw Kristi sitting on the grass a few feet away knotting a chain of clover blossoms together. While I watched, she laid the flowers at the angel's feet and sat back, her head tilted, to study their effect.

Kristi glanced up, saw me looking at her, and tried to smile. Her face was still streaked with tears. "I thought she might like some flowers," she said. "Maybe we can get some nicer ones and bring them to her tomorrow."

All around us birds and insects chirped and scolded. The summer breeze rustled the leaves of the holly tree, and from outside the graveyard came the sounds of cars and the voices of children playing in the park across the street.

"Roses," I said, thinking of the fragrance of Louisa's twilight world. "She'd like roses."

At the sound of footsteps, Kristi and I looked up, startled.

"You're right. Louisa was always partial to roses," Miss Cooper said. Giving me a bouquet of pink and yellow roses, she added, "Put these on the child's grave for me."

Taking the flowers, I laid them carefully at the angel's feet next to Kristi's clover chain. Their colors brightened the ivy.

"I'd have come sooner," Miss Cooper said, "but I didn't realize how tired I was. I sat down to rest and before I knew it, I was sound asleep."

She sighed, and gazed at the little angel. "I had a dream," Miss Cooper said. "About Louisa. I was in her yard the way it used to look and she was there, too, only she wasn't sick. She was so happy, all smiles, and I could hardly speak I was so surprised. She came to me and kissed me."

Miss Cooper touched her cheek lightly and smiled. "She forgave me."

"I had a dream like that once about my father," I said.

"I think it's their way," Miss Cooper said. "Their

way of telling you not to fret about them, to let them go."

We all were silent then. A bluejay scolded from somewhere in the treetops and a catbird called from the holly tree. Across the street, the children's voices rose and fell.

"Were you angry when Louisa died?" I asked.

Miss Cooper frowned and her mouth worked on the words before she spoke. "It shames me to say it," she admitted, "but I was mad at her for dying before I had a chance to give the doll back. And for leaving me without a friend."

She was silent for a moment. "Louisa died early in the morning," she went on, her voice shaking a little. "Mama told me at breakfast, and Papa said it was lucky for me that the Lord always took the good children first and left the ones like me for the devil to claim when he saw fit."

"What an awful thing to say." I stared at Miss Cooper, unable to imagine anyone having a father so cruel.

The old woman shrugged. "I was a bad girl, you know that yourself, but I've kept the devil waiting a long time, haven't I?"

She stared at the angel for a few seconds, her face softened by the shadows the holly tree cast over it. "But Louisa, she was a good little creature, and maybe Papa was right. She didn't suffer very long before the Lord took her."

Neither Kristi nor I spoke, so Miss Cooper went on, her old eyes fixed on the angel's face. "This is the first time I've been here since the burial. I couldn't come before, couldn't bear thinking about Louisa and that doll, knowing I'd made her unhappy. But now, well, she's got no cause to hate me."

The bluejay cried out over our heads and flew away, a flash of color in the shade. Miss Cooper leaned on her cane, as still as the angel she regarded. Then she looked down at Kristi and me. "I felt bad all these years," she said. "I'd see the cat, I'd hear Louisa crying every July, but I never thought I could give the doll back and make things right."

Slowly Miss Cooper reached out and touched our heads, first mine, then Kristi's. "I've got you girls to thank for showing me the way," she whispered.

Miss Cooper straightened up then and brushed a strand of white hair out of her eyes. For a second I remembered how she'd looked at Louisa's bedside, a little girl no older than I was.

"Well, it's powerful hot, isn't it?" Miss Cooper's voice rose to its normal level. "Why don't we walk on back home and have a nice cold glass of lemonade? I made it fresh before I left the house."

Silently Kristi and I looked at each other. Then we

followed Miss Cooper down the gravel path and out into the sunny street.

"What kind of cookies do you like?" I heard Miss Cooper ask Kristi, but I didn't listen to her answer. I was too busy thinking about what Miss Cooper had said about her dream. Had Daddy been giving me a message, too?

Chapter 20

At Peace

IT WAS A LONG slow walk back to Homewood Road, and Miss Cooper's living room felt cool after the heat of the sun. While the old woman went out to the kitchen to fix our drinks, Kristi and I sat side by side on an antique sofa. Its cushions were hard and slippery, and I felt like a child in an old-fashioned book as I listened to the tick tock of a grandfather's clock in the corner.

Kristi brought me back to the present when she nudged me and whispered, "Where's Max?"

I looked around uneasily, but I didn't see the dog. "Maybe he's outside," I said, but as I spoke I heard the click click of Max's toenails trailing behind Miss Cooper as she entered the room carrying a tray.

When Max saw Kristi and me, his number-one enemies, sitting in his living room, he raised his lip, showing a bit of mottled gum and an ugly yellow tooth. He growled softly, and Miss Cooper nudged him with her toe.

"Shush," she warned him. "These girls are my guests today, so you behave yourself, mister."

Max rolled his eyes at her and crawled under a table. Making himself comfortable, he devoted his attention to me. One false move, he seemed to say, and I'll bite off your leg.

Ignoring Max, Miss Cooper handed Kristi and me each a glass of lemonade and offered us a plate heaped with sugar cookies. While we ate, she talked about Louisa and how they'd played in the garden together.

"She had a little tea set her Papa gave her, tiny cups and saucers made out of china so fine the light showed through when you held it up to the sun. Her aunt would fix weak tea and cookies and what a feast we'd have." Miss Cooper sighed and shook her head.

"Those were the happiest times of my life, sitting there by the fountain, playing with Louisa. Then I had to go and ruin it all by stealing the doll. I don't feel so bad now, but I still wish I'd been nicer to that poor little child."

The grandfather's clock chimed one o'clock, and in the silence following, we heard Kristi's mother calling her.

"I'd better see what she wants," Kristi said

Carefully we handed Miss Cooper our empty glasses and stood up to leave. "Thank you for the lemonade and cookies," I said as I followed Kristi to the front door.

"Come and see me again," Miss Cooper said. "I think we're going to get along better, you and I, but I still don't want to see that cat of yours out in the yard scaring my birds."

She smiled at us both and stood in the doorway as we ran down the porch steps. Max barked once, but I heard Miss Cooper shush him again while Kristi and I left the yard.

Before she went into her house, Kristi turned to me. "Miss Cooper sure has gotten friendly," she said.

"It's because of Anna Maria," I said.

Kristi nodded. "She doesn't feel bad about Louisa any more." Then she frowned and kicked at a clump of chicory. "If only Louisa hadn't died," she muttered.

I looked past Kristi at the sky and the clouds and the leaves of the maple tree rustling in the breeze. "Maybe death is too big to change," I said slowly. "If Louisa had grown up and had children, the whole world could be different somehow. But giving a doll back, that's only a little thing. All it changed is Miss Cooper."

"And it didn't change her whole life," Kristi said.

"It just made her feel better, made her nicer."

"So even though we didn't save Louisa's life, we helped Miss Cooper," I said.

"Maybe that's what Louisa wanted," Kristi added, saying out loud the very thing I was thinking. "To help Carrie."

We stared at each other, and I thought of the note Carrie had buried with Anna Maria. "Please forgive me, I am sorrie." All these years, had Louisa been trying to tell Carrie she was forgiven?

"Kristi, where have you been?" Brian was staring at us from the back door. "Didn't you hear Mom calling you?"

"I'm coming, I'm coming." Kristi ran across the grass and up the porch steps. Before darting inside, she yelled to me, "I'll come over later, and we can do something. Okay?"

As the door slammed shut behind Kristi, I looked up and saw Mom on the porch. "Don't you want some lunch, Ashley?"

I nodded and climbed the steps, suddenly anxious to tell Mom everything.

*

While Mom fixed tuna salad sandwiches, I filled our glasses with iced tea and thought about what I wanted to say.

"You're awfully quiet, Ashley," Mom said as we sat

down at the table. "You haven't quarreled with Miss Cooper again, have you?"

I shook my head. "Just the opposite," I said. "I think Miss Cooper and I are going to be friends now."

Mom stared at me and I smiled at her. "Remember the doll Kristi and I found in the garden?" I asked her.

"How could I forget something that upset you so much?"

"Well, I tried to tell you the doll didn't belong to Miss Cooper, but you gave it to her anyway."

"I had to, Ashley. The doll was a valuable antique, and you found it in Miss Cooper's garden. I couldn't let you keep it, not when she said it was hers." Mom took a sip of her iced tea, but her eyes didn't leave mine.

"Well, let me tell you a story, okay?" I leaned across the table toward her and took a deep breath. "Once there was a little girl named Louisa," I began, "and she had a doll named Anna Maria."

As I continued, Mom didn't say a word. Her sandwich lay on her plate, half-finished. The ice slowly melted in her glass, but she sat still and listened.

"Now Miss Cooper is free," I finished. "She still feels bad about Louisa dying, but she knows it isn't her fault, and she knows Louisa forgave her." I looked at Mom, waiting for her to say something, but the only sound was the refrigerator humming behind me.

"What I've been thinking about is Daddy," I said finally, "and that last time I saw him in the hospital. And how bad I feel because I didn't kiss him before he died."

I started crying then, and in a couple of seconds I was on Mom's lap and she was hugging me tight. "Ashley, Ashley," she whispered, "why didn't you tell me what was bothering you?"

"I didn't want you to know I didn't kiss him," I sobbed.

Mom held me tighter. She was crying too. "Kissing couldn't save Daddy, Ashley," she said. "Nothing could. Not all the love in the world."

"I know that now. I saw Carrie kiss Louisa, and it didn't change anything. But still, it must have hurt his feelings, Mom. He must have died wondering why I'd stopped loving him."

"Oh, Ashley, when you said good-bye to him he was so drugged with pain killers, he didn't know what you said or did." She stroked my hair back from my face, drying my tears with her hand. "He knew you loved him," she whispered, "and he knew I loved him."

"I was afraid to get close to him," I said. "He didn't look like Daddy anymore."

Mom nodded. "All that was left of him were his eyes. And they were so blue, bluer than the sky."

"But Mom, the worst thing is I was angry at him. It wasn't just that I was scared, it was also because I was mad." I started crying again. "How could I have been so mad? He didn't die on purpose."

Mom sighed. "I was mad, too, Ashley."

"You were?" I stared at her.

"Of course I was. Most people are angry when somebody they love dies." She hugged me again. "We should have talked more, Ashley. I should have realized you were feeling the same things I was."

"I had a dream about Daddy a few nights ago," I told her. "He was happy and strong and he told me everything was all right. Miss Cooper had the same kind of dream about Louisa, and she said it was Louisa's way of telling her not to fret about her."

"I have dreams about Daddy, too," Mom said, "just like that."

"Then maybe Miss Cooper's right – maybe Daddy's telling us not to worry about him."

"I know he wouldn't want us to worry," Mom said. "He loved us too much to want us to be unhappy because he's gone. And he'd understand about our being angry."

I closed my eyes and clung to Mom. We were both silent, and I was sure she was remembering Daddy too – not the way he was in the hospital when he was dying, but in the days before he got sick. We'd be able to talk about Daddy now, I thought, without crying.

*

Much later, long after dark, long after I'd gone to bed, I woke up. Oscar was sitting on the windowsill looking out into the night. I knelt beside him and pressed my face against the screen, trying to see what he saw. Moonlight and shadow patterned the lawn with silver and ebony, and the old garden sweetened the air with the fragrance of honeysuckle and roses.

There was no sign of Snowball, though. "You'll never see him again," I told Oscar, knowing it was true. Like Louisa, the white cat was at peace.

Then, from the other side of the hedge, from Louisa's yard, I thought I heard a child laughing, but the sound was so faint it could have been anything — the clink of glass, a distant car radio, someone's television.

I looked at Oscar, and he looked at me, his ears pricked, his eyes wide. Then he butted his head against my face and purred, and I lay back down. Still purring, Oscar curled up beside me and I drifted off to sleep, dreaming of Louisa playing happily in the garden with Anna Maria.

MARY DOWNING HAHN

Wait Till
Helen
Comes

a ghost story

1

---✦---

"YOU'VE BOUGHT a church?" Michael and I looked up from the pile of homework covering most of the kitchen table. I was in the middle of writing a poem for Mr. Pelowski's English class, and Michael was working his way happily through twenty math questions.

Mom filled a kettle with water and put it on the stove. Her cheeks were pink from the March wind, and so was the tip of her nose. "You and Molly will love it," she promised. "It's exactly the sort of place Dave and I have been looking for all winter. There's a carriage house for him to use as a pottery workshop and space in the choir loft for me to set up a studio. It's perfect."

"But how can we live in a church?" Michael persisted, refusing to be won over by her enthusiasm.

"Oh, it's not really a church anymore," Mom said. "Some people from Philadelphia bought it last year and built an addition on the side for living quarters. They were going to set up an antique store in the actual church, but, after doing all that work, they decided they didn't like living in the country after all."

"It's out in the country?" I frowned at the little cat I was doodling in the margin of my notebook paper.

Mom smiled and gazed past me, out our kitchen window and into Mrs. Overton's window directly across the alley. I had a feeling she was seeing herself standing in front of an easel, working on one of her huge oil paintings, far from what she called the "soul-killing life of the city." She has a maddening habit of drifting away into her private dream world just when you need her most.

"Where *is* the church?" I asked loudly.

"Where is it?" Mom poured boiling water into her cup and added honey. "It's in Holwell, Maryland, not far from the mountains. It's beautiful. Just beautiful. The perfect place for painting and potting."

"But what about Molly and me? What are we supposed to do while you and Dave paint and make pottery?" Michael asked.

"You promised I could be in the enrichment program this summer," I said, thinking about the creative writing class I was planning to take. "Will I still be able to?"

"Yes, and what about Science Club?" Michael asked. "I'm already signed up for it. Mr. Phillips is going to take us to the Aquarium and the Science Center and even to the Smithsonian in Washington."

Mom sighed and shook her head. "I'm afraid you two will have to make other plans for summer. We'll be moving in June, and I can't possibly drive all the way back to Baltimore every day."

"But I've been looking forward to Science Club all year!" Michael's voice rose, and I could tell he was trying hard not to cry.

"You'll have plenty of woods to explore," Mom said calmly. "Just think of all the wildlife you can observe and the insects you can add to your collection. Why, the day Dave and I were there, we saw a raccoon, a possum, a woodchuck, and dozens of squirrels." Mom leaned across the table, smiling, hoping to convince Michael that he was going to love living in a church way out in the country, miles away from Mr. Phillips and Science Club.

But Michael wasn't easy to convince. Slumping down in his chair, he mumbled, "I'd rather stay in Baltimore, even if I never see anything but cockroaches, pigeons, and rats."

"Oh, for heaven's sake, Michael!" Mom looked exasperated. "You're ten years old. Act like it!"

As Michael opened his mouth to defend himself, Heather appeared in the kitchen doorway, responding, no doubt, to her built-in radar for detecting trouble. Her pale gray eyes roved from Mom to Michael, then to me, and back again to Mom. From the expression on her face, I imagined she was hoping to witness bloodshed, screams, a ghastly scene of domestic violence.

"Why, Heather, I was wondering where you were!" Mom turned to her, infusing her voice with enthusiasm again. "Guess what? Your daddy and I have found a new place for us to live, way out in the country. Won't that be fun?" She gave Heather a dazzling Romper-Room smile and reached out to embrace her.

With the skill of a cat, Heather sidestepped Mom's arms and peered out the kitchen window. "Daddy's home," she announced without looking at us.

"Oh, no, I forgot to put the casserole in the oven!" Mom ran to the refrigerator and pulled out a concoction of eggplant, cheese, tomatoes, and bulgur and shoved it into the oven just as

Dave opened the back door, bringing a blast of cold March air into the room with him.

After giving Mom a hug and a kiss, he swooped Heather up into his arms. "How's my girl?" he boomed.

Heather twined her arms possessively around his neck and smiled coyly. "They were fighting," she said, darting a look at Michael and me.

Dave glanced at Mom, and she smiled and shook her head. "We were just discussing our big move to the country, that's all. Nobody was *fighting*, Heather." Mom turned on the cold water and began rinsing lettuce leaves for a salad.

"I don't like it when they fight." Heather tightened her grip on Dave's neck.

"Come on, Michael." I stood up and started gathering my books and papers together. "Let's finish our homework downstairs."

"Dinner will be ready in about half an hour," Mom called after us as we started down the basement steps.

As soon as we were safely out of everybody's hearing range, I turned to Michael. "What are we going to do?"

He flopped down on the old couch in front of the television. "Nothing. It's too late, Molly. They've bought the church and we're moving there. Period."